THE ENCRYPTION GAME

A Dr. Scott James Thriller

GLENN SHEPARD

MYSTERY HOUSE

COPYRIGHT ©2016 BY GLENN Shepard. All rights reserved. Except as permitted under the United States of America Copyright Act of 1976, no part of this publication may be reproduced or distributed in any form or by any means or stored in a database or retrieval system without the prior written permission of the publisher.

www.glennshepardauthor.com

Mystery House Publishing, Inc.

Newport News, VA

ISBN 0-9971349-2-5

ISBN 978-0-9971349-2-6

Cover and interior design by Annie Biggs and Scott Line

Printed in the United States of America.

THE ENCRYPTION GAME

Chapter 1

Day 1
The Tomb of Kim Il-Sung
Kumsusan Palace of the Sun
Pyongyang, North Korea
8:22 a.m.

THE DEAD AND EMBALMED body of "The Dear Leader" of North Korea lay under a polished dome of crystal glass. Omar Farok stood there, transfixed by the sheer splendor of it all. This was what he wanted for himself. He wanted to be worshiped long after he was dead. Here, in the capital of North Korea, he'd found the proper respect given to a great leader. The massive tomb of the founder of North Korea lay in a spectacular mausoleum, a gigantic building that had once been the capital's congressional complex. The North Koreans had turned it into a fabulous palace, spending perhaps as much as a hundred million dollars to make it into a sacred place. Omar could picture something like this for himself, but bigger, more splendid, with sparkling gold glitter on all of it.

He'd been dusted before he'd entered the inner sanctum, the huge room where the tomb actually lay. They had a blower at the entrance and Farok was made to stand under it for a moment to remove any particle that might soil this holiest of places. Here, in front of the Father of North Korea, there would be no dust!

Farok's head swam at the idea of such hero-worship, and then suddenly, annoyingly, someone began to roll a cart or a piece of equipment loudly across the marble floor. Startled, Farok looked around. Who would be so crazy as to make such a noise in this colossus of solitude? Or was it a special effect? Was there some kind of motorized display for tourists who were lucky enough to make it to the inner sanctum? Then Omar began to realize that the rolling noise and the creaking of wheels were in reality the sounds of the gigantic tomb itself, sliding across the floor.

The megalithic crystal tomb kept moving, slowly, heavily, and at Omar Farok's feet a gap opened in the floor where the massive sarcophagus had been. Clearly, there was a chamber beneath the tomb. The opening widened and light began to penetrate the rectangular hole in the floor. The face of a severe-looking military officer appeared. He was standing at the top of what looked like stairs, and he was looking right at Farok. The officer wore the huge, balloon-style hat that they all wore and the colorful, yellow and brown collar marker of a full colonel. He looked Farok in the eye and suddenly barked, "Come! You! Come! Now!"

Farok could see better into to the chamber now and he could see that behind the colonel stood several soldiers, standing at attention on a series of steps. The cement stairs disappeared down the long corridor, and the North Korean troops stood against the walls, stiffly carrying heavily-polished Kalashnikov automatic rifles.

Omar Farok now knew why his body guards had been stopped at the entrance of the inner sanctum. He had traveled with only three of his henchmen specifically because he'd been told that only four people at a time were allowed in to see the tomb. But Omar had been sent through the duster alone and then guided directly in to see the tomb by himself. This wasn't a random occurrence.

The stern colonel at the lip of the tunnel waved so sharply that the sleeves of his starched jacket popped against his arm with each violent gesture. *Pop. Pop.* *"YOU! COME!"*

Omar hesitated. The tunnel under the tomb represented a fifty-fifty proposition. Maybe the North Koreans knew of his obvious genius and wanted to work with him. Or maybe the North Koreans were going to swallow him into their underground network and he would never be seen again.

Farok looked around the pristine room for a brief instant. The tour guides and the honor guard stood to either side, stoically watching the scene. There was no emotion whatsoever. How many had they seen disappear this way?

Farok wondered.

"COME," the colonel said, in English. "NOW!"

Farok edged forward slightly.

The colonel waved to two soldiers nearby to grab Farok and force him to comply, and they obeyed with precision. The tour guides turned their backs and began leaving.

Farok immediately knew the only thing to do was to smile, which he did, unconvincingly.

Stepping forward, Omar Farok began to descend into the chamber below the great tomb of The Dear Leader. The colonel grasped him by the elbow and pulled him down slightly just as the tomb began closing. The creaking of the heavy concrete grated loudly overhead as Farok stepped from one level to the other, down, down, down, down. He then heard, very distinctly, the sudden stop of the giant marble slab, closing the entrance above him. The tunnel was sealed.

Chapter 2

Day 1
Virginia Peninsula Regional Jail
Williamsburg, Virginia
7:00 p.m.

THE FIRST DAY IN jail was a nightmare. They were already calling me "Oswald." One of my interrogators actually called what I did an "Oswald-Kennedy-style assassination."

I was accused of capital murder, but even more than that was the fact that the killing was done with a sniper rifle, a powerful one at long range, in a large public space with lots of people around. Like Lee Harvey. "A Lee Harvey Oswald-style, long range sniper shot."

I did kill him, I admit that. But this was no political assassination. The man I killed was a terrorist. Yet, I am now told the man was not a terrorist, he carried no bomb,

and was a humanitarian known throughout the world.
The parade of inquisitors was endless. For twelve continuous hours they questioned me, men and women introduced as being from the FBI, the Virginia state police, the James City police, the Secret Service, and a half dozen other agencies—even a US Senator's aide.

My conscience was clear. I sat tall and bounced the answers back to them. I was never intimidated. I told the truth. My answers could be summarized in four statements:

1. There is an organization that is involved in the most extraordinary schemes and operations that can possibly be imagined. It is loosely affiliated with ISIS. Only a handful of people know of it, and I am one of those who know.

2. The leader of this organization is Omar Farok. He is going to attack America, and in a way you'd never expect—that's his trademark.

3. I am positive the man I killed was the man I know only as "Emmanuel," a terrorist who worked for Omar Farok.

4. I am not a terrorist myself. I am not an "operative." I'm not anything—a cultist, an anarchist—nothing, and neither am I mentally disturbed in any manner.

But after the first five hours of questioning, I was tired. Many times I'd functioned without mental or physical limitations in all-nighters at my job in the operating room. But this was different. I became more tired under the relentless questioning than I could even imagine. It was then that I realized how many prisoners over the years could have succumbed to giving a confession just to stop the brutal barrage of questions, and the reality that so many who signed confessions under duress were never

The Encryption Game

given due process of law.

I didn't want to seem uncooperative. I didn't want to avoid the questions. I didn't want to seem guilty. Early in the interrogation, I asked for my lawyer. They countered by asking if I was refusing to cooperate. Then they said they were having trouble getting him on the phone. They said it was late. Again they accused me of not cooperating.

I told you people: I killed a terrorist.

Every question had an accusatory element and the demand that I tell the truth and confess my deranged behavior. Everything had a bargain on the end of it, too. If I confessed to everything I would get a life sentence rather than death. If I confessed to everything I would only get twenty years in prison instead of life, or a mental institution as opposed to prison, and on and on. They said I "need to consider these things," and "you should stop playing games and come clean and tell us everything right now."

Games. It was all part of an insane game, one that I didn't want to play, one that was always getting worse and worse as each week passed.

I will confess everything here. I'll come clean. I'm a regular guy who has been dragged in to a conspiracy to attack the United States. I'm a doctor, a plastic surgeon, to be precise.

Or, I *was* a doctor—a cranial-facial expert.

But then a terrorist targeted the hospital I worked in, and from that event I became involved in a thing that I still cannot figure out. Have you ever seen a poor, unwitting guy in the documentary on TV, a guy who gets dragged into it all? That's me.

Now I'm an informant, an insider, an observer, a victim, an "asset," a "known quantity." A *doctor?* Ha! I might as well be working for the CIA! I spent my life fixing people's faces—now I'm a news item, a headline, "the guy who shot…" The guy on TV.
I don't want to be a part of any of this. I have to clear my name and tell my story or I'm going to spend the rest of my life in a stinking prison cell, or, possibly, be executed. But what happens when only one guy knows the truth? Or, in my case, what happens when you're the only person *telling* the truth?

The truth is that I was present at the arrival of the group of Syrian refugees who came to Virginia a couple of days ago. It was all over the news media. The President was there, as was the Governor. They brought them in for a staged event in Williamsburg. I was close by, in Jackson City, North Carolina, and I had reason to believe that this organization, the one that hit my hospital, was planning a bombing. I did my patriotic duty. I told the FBI what I thought. These people have been asking me for information for months, and I've given them everything I know. Like I said, this terrorist organization, led by Omar Farok, tried to bomb my hospital and in the process tried to kill me. I actually know some of these people. I've met them face-to-face.

I told the Feds that I wanted to come to the ceremony in Williamsburg as an observer. There were a hundred or so Syrians who were going to arrive, and security was going to be tight. I talked my FBI contacts into letting me work with the security detail. When we got there, they gave me a pair of binoculars and stationed me next to one of the rooftop snipers. It took me all of about two minutes to spot one of Farok's organization: The man known only to me as Emmanuel.

He was tall, six-one, and a head higher than the Syrians he accompanied. As a plastic surgeon, I could pick out and recognize the contours of his face, his minor facial flaws, the slightly bulging eyes and the receding chin which he consciously corrected by pushing his lower jaw outward. I also noticed, through my binoculars, that his jacket bulged, noticeably. He was wearing a bomb vest. He was only thirty feet away from the President, who was making a speech.

There was no time to think, no time to consider what might happen. I took the sniper's rifle and made the shot myself.

Each time I close my eyes to picture Emmanuel at the President's speech in Williamsburg, I see something bulky beneath his clothes. Before I shot, I interpreted this as a vest loaded with explosives. Could that have been a bullet proof vest instead?

I needed to see one of the "death photos" of Emmanuel. That, for me, was Point One: I needed to know if I really killed him. Or did body armor protect him from death?

I keep thinking about the moment I pulled the trigger. Emmanuel fell immediately and I saw people rush to him. My last view of Emmanuel was blocked by those moving to assist him.

There is a complication in all this that shouldn't be there. It shouldn't even be a consideration, but the world is a circus now, so I might as well get used to this complication: The problem is that years ago I wrote a paper about The Kennedy Assassination. It wasn't much. It was just the results of a little experiment I tried. It wasn't even published or really known until some bigwig wrote about it in The New Yorker. They say you can learn a lot by reading that magazine ...

They're already calling me "Oswald," because it was a shot made by a guy in the window of an old building. They're claiming I'm just like Lee Harvey Oswald, you know: "A loner," and "a troubled past," and the idea that I have a "mysterious international girlfriend."

Troubled past? What the hell are they talking about?! I'd never been in trouble a day in my life, until ...

There's another problem in all this: I know the man I killed. Emmanuel was a suicide bomber. Like I said, I know some of these people, but it's purely against my will.

I did shoot him. I don't care who knows that. He was about to detonate a bomb that would have killed the President of the United States as well as thousands of people attending the Syrian Refugee Welcoming Ceremony at Williamsburg, Virginia.

I saved thousands of lives by shooting Emmanuel.

But in the public's eyes, I am a political assassin. I'm a single *BOOM* in a public square.

I spent the night in solitary confinement. I slept in a claustrophobic, eight-by-four-foot cell, on a half-inch pad that they called a bed.

Is that what happened to Oswald? Did he wake up like me one day—the "guy in the paper?" Am I going crazy? Are they getting to me? I'm a Doctor. I just want to do what I do best: Surgery.

Chapter 3

In The Tunnel
Kumsusan Palace of the Sun
Pyongyang, North Korea
8:26 a.m.

OMAR AND THE NORTH Korean colonel walked swiftly. The steps of the tunnel were too long to walk on in a natural way. They seemed to be custom made for the inhabitants of the underground to run on. The colonel galloped down the steps with Omar willing himself forward, clumsily.

After only a few seconds, the colonel said over his shoulder to the following Farok, "We received your encrypted message."

This was the only reason that Farok had not run for his life when the tomb opened, not that it would have

17

helped. He'd sent a message to General Sae Ban Sook, Chief of Military Intelligence, a week earlier, saying that he was traveling to Pyongyang to take in the glorious sights, including the tomb of The Dear Leader, and he was in a position to offer the North Korean government an extraordinary opportunity.

He'd made overtones to the North Koreans for years. They were in the same business, essentially: Hating America. Farok loved how the Kims had crushed all dissent in their country, how they threatened the Americans every chance they got, how they did such a good job of supporting the persecuted of the world, like Qaddafi and Mubarak.

So another offer to do business didn't really stir interest among the North Koreans. He'd sent messages like this before, so it was hardly a surprise for anyone. But it was the *way* in which he'd sent the message that had elicited the attention of the North Korean high command. He'd encrypted the message in such a way that only North Korean intelligence would be able to decrypt it, a fact that made officials in Pyongyang believe that Farok had figured out how to decrypt at least a small portion of their own classified messages. Farok had known that it would be seen a seriously provocative gesture.

Considering who he was, disappearing into the bowels of a dictatorship wasn't that unusual for Omar Farok. He worked with them all, the dictators, the freelance arms dealers, the private armies, the terrorists. His view was that it was all part of destiny, that great world events and small happenstance, both, were pulling him forward toward his inevitable rise to power. He would be the leader

The Encryption Game

of ISIS someday—and someday *soon*, at that. This fact was obvious, or at least it was in his eyes, and so it was natural that he would be taken to the inner corridors of the world's great powers.

Omar had of course nurtured a reputation for being a cut above. He'd started out by advertising himself as a "Prince from The Sudan." He was indeed a distant relative of the Egyptian King of the 1950s, Farouk, although that dynasty had long-since been dissolved. Nevertheless, he'd been born into a land-owning family, and raised in opulent luxury, even if it wasn't exactly royalty.

Farok was small, with even smaller features that made him look disturbingly rat-like. He pictured himself, however, as being just one step away from looking like the dashing Egyptian actor, Omar Sharif. Unlike the handsome Sharif, though, Farok's facial hair was too patchy to sport an impressive mustache, so he'd gone to the finest, most discreet salon in Beverly Hills, to have a respectable one weaved. It was a hair-and-make-up utopia out there in LA. They really knew what they were doing. Omar liked his weaved-and-glued mustache so much that he'd added a little wax to the ends, to give it more character.

He'd tried everything he could to improve his appearance: platform shoes, an abundance of expensive jewelry, a hairpiece. The Saudi Royals walked around in keffiyehs, so Omar had taken to wearing a headdress and thobe. It made him look more royal, he thought. The problem with the keffiyeh and thobe was that when you told people you were a "Prince," they took you seriously. He'd kept the robes, but had changed his title to the slightly less ostentatious "Emir."

As they hurried downward, Omar noticed that the tunnel was conspicuously well-heated, an important consideration during the bitter North Korean winters. He also noticed the silence. The colonel said nothing and the troops stood at attention, staring forward.

Farok knew all the rogues, all except one, the North Korean state. He was the biggest player in the world if you wanted to sell black market oil. After his family fortune, this was where most of his millions had come from. ISIS was his most active client. Selling their oil and bringing in millions to the caliphate had raised him to a certain status. But he was still on the outside, untrusted by the fighters in Syria and Iraq. Farok hoped to exploit his financial connections and prowess to ascend to the throne, to the top of ISIS, where he belonged—where a man of his intellect and charm deserved to be.

There was only one stumbling block to destiny: He would have to prove himself all-powerful. He would have to prove that he could launch a stunning attack on America, a massive blow, unlike any other. Then those crude, ungrateful jihadists ruling in northern Syria, the ones who were running the caliphate—who had never shown him the proper respect—then even *they* would have to admit that Omar Farok was a great man.

Omar liked the simple-mindedness that came from having a single goal that blocked out all other considerations. Just make the biggest attack, he thought, then he'd be on top.

At last, the tunnel stopped descending, and Farok walked alongside the swiftly-moving colonel down a cement corridor. Polished troops stood at attention all the

The Encryption Game

way down. It was hardly necessary to call attention to the fact that down here, only a few were allowed to speak. Silence hung heavy. Farok knew better than to make small talk.

At the end of the tunnel there was a table. "The End" was a good way to describe it. The tunnel seemed to stop, to make a dead end, and there, seated, were four army officers.

The colonel who had accompanied Farok didn't break stride. He walked swiftly around one end of the table and took his seat in the center. Farok as now standing in front of five officers, total, all of them looking very business-like.

The colonel, in his very good English, began to read from a document. "Dated October 6, 'My organization wishes to discuss an opportunity of great strategic importance with your government.'" The colonel put down the page he'd been reading and said, "Now, what is this matter about?"

Farok noticed that there was something strange about the line-up of officers. There were no generals. There was the colonel, a major who was clearly the colonel's assistant, and three captains. That was it. There wasn't a senior officer present. More than that, there was something wrong with the officers themselves. One of the captains, for example, was an older, distinguished-looking gentleman. This guy was obviously the oldest "captain" in the army. Farok began to wonder if this was perhaps a general in disguise. "I had planned to discuss this matter with General Sook," Farok said, in the most off-hand, polite way he could manage.

The elderly captain spoke up suddenly. "What have you got?"

"A plan."

The man hadn't expected that answer and he hesitated for a moment. Then he smiled. "What about this little man? What is his name? Scott James? Do you think you can manage to get around him this time?" The line of officers exploded in laughter, slapping each other on the backs, guffawing, stomping their feet. Farok turned red and began to shake in rage. The intelligence world had had a field day with the fact that his organization had been defeated by a "small town doctor." Somehow, it seemed, an unknown, untrained man had managed to shoot Farok's private assassin at the last minute. The embarrassment was almost too much to take.

The old captain was laughing so hard that he suddenly had a fit of coughing. The others started to calm down. Farok jumped at the momentary pause. "A single bomb could destroy America, if used properly."

"Nonsense," the elderly captain answered, trying to catch his breath. "America is too big, too vast."

"No, General... uh... *Captain*. I do not speak of killing the body of the giant. It is, as you said, too big to kill. We can kill its brain. We can kill it electronically."

The board of officers sat quietly and let the scenario play out. Farok and the "Captain" knew the game, so there was no more need for a total charade. The captain sat back slightly in his chair and pulled out a pack of cigarettes. "You mean the electrical scenario," he said, as he fished out a smoke and lit up.

For the first time, Farok noticed that there was a light

The Encryption Game

bulb protruding from the far corner of the tabletop. It was strange. The tunnel was well-lit. The North Koreans had gone so far as to use indirect light to cut down on the glare inside the cement rooms. Nevertheless, at one end of the polished, well-made table, there was a simple light fixture screwed into the surface. The white bulb stood up like a sore thumb.

Farok felt like the elderly captain's question was an invitation to elaborate, so he continued: "Yes. 'The electrical scenario.' Electro Magnetic Pulse. If a nuclear device were to be detonated at the right altitude and in the right geographical location, the pulse created by the release of energy could burn out every weak electrical connection in the entire eastern United States. It would cause a total blackout. It's a feasible concept."

"We are aware that this is..." The elderly captain searched for the word that Farok had used, but gave up and simply said, "We know it works. But so do the Americans. They know that EMP is a threat. They are moving their sensitive circuitry underground."

"But they haven't moved much, and it's all been military in nature. A single bomb could produce enough of an energy pulse to overload the circuitry of all of the civilian systems, the flight-control centers, hospitals, the mainframe computers of thousands of their corporations, their Internet servers, everything. There are millions of weak connections. Even if only twenty-five percent were broken, the Americans would lose all control of the eastern part of the country."

"What then, Mr. Farok? What then?"

Farok resisted the urge to tell the Korean officer to call

him by his preferred title, "Emir." He hated being called by a commoner's title, "Mr."

For the elderly North Korean, it was clear that Omar was just another case of a fanatic who was itching to die for his cause and didn't understand that others weren't in such a hurry. These people never understood military reality, the old man thought. He was enjoying his cigarette. "Mr. Farok, if we explode a bomb anywhere near America, they will launch their missiles and bring total destruction to everything." He swept his hand in a wide arc, "everything" obviously meant "North Korea."

"Not if they think that ISIS did it."

The smoking man hesitated again. That was two answers he hadn't expected. "So," he continued, "you've destroyed the electronics of the east coast of America. They will just rebuild." He made a fist and put it to his own face and then shook his head. "It wouldn't be the knock out punch."

"With a real Electro Magnetic Pulse, a well-planned EMP, we can destroy the Americans' ability to control their ground forces in the east. We can destroy their Command and Control near their bases and weapons facilities. If we have enough troops on the ground nearby, we can penetrate their installations—"

"Troops! What troops? The Government of North Korea is not offering troops to you or anyone else! We are willing to discuss the sale of armaments, but we aren't interested in any scenario that involves our troops."

"Sir: *My* troops."

"What? What are you talking about?"

"I can have two-to-three thousand soldiers massed on

The Encryption Game

American soil at any time."

"You have three thousand men in America? We find that hard to believe."

"I can do it. I've poured all of my resources into this project. I have moles deep inside the American military."

"What do you intend to do with... What did you say? 'Two-to-three-thousand men'? Even if the Americans can only put a few regiments into action, your war will be over quite quickly and the world will still be in the place it is today, but with a vengeful, unstable America."

"This is not a war, Captain, it's a *raid*."

"A raid? I find that amusing, Mr. Farok. The use of a nuclear warhead is a raid?"

"There is a target. It is a military transit center in Virginia. We know that the Americans are moving fifty of their W-80 warheads from Georgia to Maine, and that they will stop there. They always stop there, overnight, during their trip from Georgia to Maine. It is a soft target. It is a transit center. When the warheads transit there, they're not put into vaults. A sudden, swift assault against this target—and it will fall. And with no communications, they won't know we've done it. This particular facility is near a public waterway. We can bring up my boats and get the warheads out of the country within ninety minutes. The EMP will make it virtually impossible for them to stop a well-coordinated operation. Once we've got the warheads, the balance of power in the world will be irrevocably changed. Within a month, every enemy of America will have the bomb, and you won't be implicated in any way. The balance of power as it is today will cease to exist."

"Ha! This is a fantasy! Mr. Farok, your bombs

won't work! The Americans don't transport live nuclear warheads! Nobody does!"

"You're familiar with the incident that occurred in the 2007 in North Dakota?"

"Of course I am. Everybody is."

"The Americans transported live nuclear warheads, thinking they were just obsolete cruise missiles."

"Yes. Yes. We know. Yes? So? That was an accident! It was a logistical error! As soon as the Americans discovered that they had transported live bombs there was a huge scandal. They would never do this again."

"I can make it happen again. I can manufacture this accident. My people on the inside know the paperwork. They know how to do it. They know how the live weapons were mistaken for inactive ones in the North Dakota incident. I assure you, there will be live warheads in that shipment. It's purely a matter of knowing which 'mistakes' to make in the paperwork."

"These weapons will be useless to you. They use extraordinarily complex passwords. This is unbreakable encryption, even for them. Without the codes, you'll never be able to arm the—"

"I have a mole on the inside who can get me the passwords, letter-for-letter, in real time... Captain. We can activate the warheads, once they're in our possession. I am the only one who can do this."

Silence hung in the room. The two men stared at each other. Cigarette smoke formed a haze over the table. Farok waited for the next question. He didn't want to seem needy or weak. He stood quietly and waited.

The light bulb lit.

The Encryption Game

Click.

Farok jumped a little. He stared at the bulb. At the far end of the table, a bright light had just spontaneously come on, even though no one in the room had moved a finger.

Farok slowly turned his eyes from the glowing bulb to the elderly captain. There was a weird look on the old man's face: Admiration. Or, perhaps, *satisfaction* was a better description. It was hard to tell. In his highly American-sounding accent, the smirking captain said, "Return to your hotel room. We'll be in touch."

Chapter 4

Virginia Peninsula Regional Jail
Williamsburg, Virginia
Midnight

SWEAT BROKE OUT ALL over my body. I turned in my bed. I tossed back and forth. I struggled to awaken. But I had a mission. I must find the bomb and defuse it. A bomb will explode and kill the US President and hundreds of people! There was a crowd of people, standing, looking, listening, and waiting for the man on stage to begin speaking. I tossed and turned on the narrow shelf that stuck from the wall, with a thin mat covering it. I struggled to open my eyes, but never succeeded. All was dark again. A peaceful sleep. That's what I needed in my first night in this hellhole of a jail. Then I remembered it. I knew I was sleeping.

I was at that point where you start to suspect it's a dream. But I couldn't wake up. I ran through them, the crowd of people, shoving, pushing, throwing them aside... looking for someone among the Syrian refugees... someone with a bomb... in a suicide vest... someone with no fear of dying... and orders to detonate the bomb. Jesus, God, those innocents... with families who will be wrecked by their deaths... I must save them!

It was slow motion. My legs were heavy. I struggled to take each step. As I moved, I turned the head of each of the Syrian refugees I passed. I looked them square in the face. There were no emotions. Just blank stares. They didn't even know I was there.

There were only fifty of them, so the papers said. But they were wrong. There were hundreds of them, maybe a thousand. The women wore hijabs, with their faces exposed, the men had brightly colored, short-sleeved shirts, with black or blue trousers. One of them had orders to kill people, my people, Americans.

My eyes were blurry. I tried to wipe the sweat from my eyes, but there was a film over them. I dug my fingernails into my eyebrows and tried to pull the blur away. I felt pain, pain that gave me joy. I let go of my face and reached for the light that blinded me, the light of consciousness, the light that would restore me to reality!

But instead I looked around. The Syrians crowded around me. I was smothered. I stood on my toes to catch my breath. Then I saw him! A black man, a head taller than the Syrians! I took a deep breath and spread my elbows, creating a space in which to move. I tried to lift my legs and move toward him. But he was a football field away from me. My legs were heavy. On second effort, I moved. The man was closer. I stepped again. He was only an arm's length away. I touched his face and turned it toward me. His eyes bulged outward, he had a strong nose, one that was perfect and needed no plastic surgery correction... the chin... there was a problem... it recessed to the point of allowing air escape as he talked... I can fix that... I fix faces... I saw the surgical instruments on the Mayo Stand in front of me... I took the electric saw and pressed the foot pedal... the oscillating blade made a loud, whirring sound. My assistant placed the suction in his mouth and suctioned away the trickle of blood that obscured the osteotomy site. In what seemed like two seconds, I'd sectioned both mandibles with a stair-step cut, pulled the jaw forward, and screwed in metal plates to maintain a perfect occlusion.

All I want is for things to be the way they were.

All I ever wanted to do was operate. I was a good surgeon. My chief said many times, "If you don't think you're the best surgeon in the world to do a particular operation, refer it to someone who is." That was my motto of life. I was the best. I never referred facial surgery. I felt a calmness as I felt myself return to a deep sleep.

I awakened with a jolt. There was Emmanuel, and his jaw remained recessed despite my good surgery. I reached for him again. I felt my heart beating rapidly. Sweat dripped into my hands. I wiped them on my T-shirt and grabbed at his shoulder. But he was across the room. I moved closer, yet, he kept moving away.

I looked up, on the roof of the Capitol Building. There was a sniper! I waved both my arms. He saw me! He turned and looked at me as I shouted, "It's Emmanuel! He'll kill the President!"

I tried to locate Emmanuel again, but he'd vanished.

The sniper waved for me to join him on the roof. I looked for a stairway to get me there, but there was none. Then I had the feeling that I could fly. I moved my body upward and I moved toward the roof. As I moved in the air I felt the excitement of a bird, flying to its nest. But my arms didn't move. I pointed both arms to the roof, and again I was in slow motion, moving, slowly moving, in the air, with no fear of falling, just joy. It took forever to complete the flight, and touch my feet on the balcony where the sniper stood.

The sniper hugged me, the President saw my flight and waved as he said, "Thanks for saving my life."

I smiled at his remark. With the President of the United States as a new friend, I'll be able to do everything I want to do. I'll build another surgical center, just like I did in Jackson City. I'll operate, and Elizabeth will again work with me in the office. The kids will be so happy.

And I'll be made whole again, doing my life's dream, with no interference from Farok.

But there was Emmanuel. In the crowd below, moving through the Syrians, closer and closer to the President. I tried to scream, but in the silent movie I was a part of, my lips moved but words did not come.

Tears gushed from my eyes. I thrashed my arms from side to side as I cried. But my mother and father were at my side. These two farmers sacrificed their lives to put me through the best schools in the world and make me the surgeon that I am. I stopped my crying and hugged them both. "I'm sorry you have to see me in this jail. I just wish..."

"Shhh," my mother said. "We're both so proud of you."

Dad grabbed me in his arms and held me. "You have been so brave, and done more for the world than they'll ever be able to appreciate. It's not what the newspapers say about you, but how you feel about yourself," he tapped his fist on his chest, "in your own heart."

The President suddenly yelled "Shoot him! Shoot that guy!" I was thrashing in my tiny bed, my body cold and my T-shirt sopping wet. I was trying to raise the sniper rifle to fire. I began the slow, arduous task of raising the rifle. At last, I felt it against my cheek. The sight dropped on Emmanuel. His hand touched his pocket. I pulled the trigger as hard as I could but it didn't move. Then I saw my parents at Emmanuel's side. That gave the strength I needed. I pulled the trigger!

Chapter 5

Day 2
Headquarters of UNESCO
Place de Fontenoy
Paris, France
2:40 p.m.

BRUMMEN YOURGI SAT ON his Louis XIV sofa and doodled on a gold framed note pad with a 1930's fountain pen. He scratched the smooth skin of his forehead and considered the situation carefully, occasionally making notes in his tiny cursive script, each letter demonstrating his perfect penmanship. He picked up his phone to make a call, hesitated, put the phone down, then got up and walked to his floor-to-ceiling bookshelves. Of all the antique books that packed his personal library, he selected *The Doors of*

Perception, by Aldous Huxley, and thumbed to the back cover to read a note. It was in his own handwriting and was headed by the title, "From a talk by Huxley to the San Francisco Medical School, 1961":

"There will be in the next generation or so a pharmacological method of making people love their servitude and producing dictatorship without tears so to speak. Producing a kind of painless concentration camp for entire societies so that people will in fact have their liberties taken away from them, but will rather enjoy it, because they will be distracted from any desire to rebel—by propaganda, or brainwashing, or brainwashing enhanced by pharmacological methods. And this seems to be the final revolution."

As he replaced the book, a fleck of lint dropped to his black suit. He walked briskly to his bathroom and took a tiny brush to remove the lint, then adjusted his black knit, square bottomed tie. Back in his office, he seated himself at the ornately carved, gold-trimmed desk that once belonged to Henry VIII. After shuffling in his straight-backed period chair, he lifted the phone and said, "Get me the American Secretary of the Navy."

Yourgi sat with his hands clasped in front of him until the phone rang. "Gene? Brummen here," he said with a heavy British accent. "By my count, I believe you owe me a favor."

"Really? I already introduced you to my beautiful daughter and took care of your little problem in Yemen."

"Your daughter is beautiful, and I do thank you for availing me of that pleasure. But I am certain that your Sailors or Marines will once again get themselves in trouble for taking indecent liberties with our French lovelies and need an insider to unlock the door to their jail cell."

The Secretary laughed and said, "Yes, yes. My men don't tolerate French Champagne and women, both at the same time. Tell me how I can assist you."

"An American is being detained in a jail just outside Williamsburg, Virginia. I personally know a gentleman who wishes to kill him when the opportunity avails, whether in jail or after his release on bond, which I am certain will happen."

The Secretary laughed again. "Which have you arranged, his bond or his assassination?"

"Well, I have followed this doctor for the past year..."

"I take it you're talking about Dr. Scott James? The man who killed UNESCO's poster boy?"

"That's right. I'd like the doctor housed in the dorm facility at Quantico. I know the 250 rooms you need for your FBI training classes are open for the semester break. If you could offer a suite for him and the two friends who help him, and use the Witness Protection clause, which is under FBI control, to place his two young kids and their grandmother, just for ten days, I'll be obligated to you."

The Secretary scratched his nose, stared into space for a second, then replied, "If it's just for ten days, I can handle it. But someday you'll have to tell me of your involvement here. And don't deny you have a special interest. I'm guessing it relates to the placement of the Muslim refugees in America..."

"Someday, over a good Bordeaux, I'll tell you, and thanks."

Chapter 6

The State Attorney General's Office
Richmond, Virginia
2:45 a.m.

TIMOTHY BUTLER SAT WITH his eyes closed, his legs propped up on his desk, and the phone cradled between his ear and shoulder. Empty paper cups filled his trash can and a steaming cup of coffee sat next to a pile of papers. He nodded off at intervals whenever the US Attorney General in DC, Eric Garret, put him on hold for extended periods of time. All the while, his secretary sat on the edge of her chair with her pen poised over her third note tablet. Two other pads, filled with her written notes, were neatly placed on the side of Butler's desk.

Butler's body jerked as Garret spoke sharply. "The President wants this case tried in federal court. I know

Governor Wilson wants this tried as a routine murder in Virginia."

Butler held his hand over the phone and shook his head. He said quietly to the receptionist, "The governor wants no part of this spectacle."

"The President sends his apologies to Governor Wilson, as he will miss all the publicity and notoriety such a trial will bring to your state..."

Butler looked at his secretary and again shook his head back and forth.

"...and he knows that routine murder trials are in the state's jurisdiction, but he wants very much for this one to be handled by the Federal Court system. We're going to try it as a capital murder case."

"Then, that's the final ruling? That Dr. James will be tried by your people?"

"That's right. It's not as clean a fit in a judicial slot as I'd like, but the President wants this. A lot. That's why I've been talking to you all these hours, trying to work this out to his liking."

Chapter 7

Day 3
Virginia Peninsula Regional Jail
7:08 a.m.

I WAS IN A wavering state of consciousness and heard my friend, Jakjak, trying to converse with me, but I didn't know what he was saying. Then I started coming out of the nightmare.

I blinked, painfully. It was morning. I was covered in sweat and blinded by the intense sunlight piercing through the thin window slit of my cell. I closed my eyes tightly and put my arm over my face, but the light still blinded me. I had to put something over that window. I sat on the side of the bed and touched the floor with my feet. I tried to stand. I couldn't do it. I felt dizzy and held on to the bed frame to keep from falling. I tried a second time, with great effort, and succeeded in standing upright.

But there was movement between me and the window. I shielded my eyes with my hand and tried to see.

There was a man at the window. I tried to focus, but the brilliant glare made it difficult.

"Who are you?" I asked.

I was surprised that the apparition answered, "A friend."

My body wavered back and forth. I felt nauseous and flopped back to a seated position on the edge of the bed.

"It's so bright in here. I can't see you."

He stepped in front of the window, just enough so that I saw the form of a man, a thin man, in a tight fitting black suit. His shirt was white and starched and his tie was dark and narrow. I tried to see his face by using both hands as a visor. The only thing I could discern was that he wore wrap-around sunglasses. But his hair was strange. He had a spiked crew cut, maybe three inches tall in the front. I couldn't be sure what his hair color was, but with the sunlight on his head, it appeared to be blonde.

"Why are you here? Who are you? Is this more questions?"

As I asked this, I realized this could be one of Farok's hired assassins. My pulse quickened. I turned to the door and tried to shout, but my voice only croaked as I yelled, "Hey! Hey! Help me! HELP!"

It was as if time stood still. I waited for the guards to barge in and dispatch this guy, but nobody appeared at the door. I made my hands into fists and tried to turn and confront him, but I felt myself falling. The ground was rushing up to me ... but the stranger put his hand under my arm and helped me back to the bed.

Afterward, he strolled back and returned to his spot in front of the window, and folded his arms across his chest.

I noticed that there was an unlit cigarette in his hand. There was something very wrong here. I said, "Please leave."

I thought I heard him chuckle.

"Why do you laugh at me?"

He lit his cigarette and inhaled, then blew the smoke toward me.

I smelled the distinct smell of pot. I took a deep breath, then inhaled again. My head began to swirl. Euphoria replaced fear. He blew smoke again, and I opened my mouth and brought even more of the stimulant into my lungs.

"Who the hell are you? What is this? Are you an inmate?"

"You're a good man, Doctor. You've helped a lot of people in your lifetime and I know you're eager to return to your life as a surgeon."

This was no inmate. The moment he said that I realized that he knew my life, my personal information, and probably the contents of my "file." I tried again to see his face, but he moved aside so the sun blinded me again.

I covered my eyes with both hands as I answered, "Yes. My life's been screwed up. Returning to the way things were before, that is my wish. If I could only go back to the way things were before ... "

He leaned to me and slowly blew the pot smoke at me and watched as I smiled in enjoyment. This guy was having good time. He wasn't like the others. He was the strangest, most carefree man I have ever encountered. It was like nothing could hurt him.

"What's your name?" I asked.

He smiled as though my question was something a child would ask.

"Who do you work for? CIA? FBI?"

"Do you want to go back to the way things were? Permanently?"

I spoke without considering my words, "I'd do anything to return to my former life."

"Anything?"

"Yes, anything."

"Then I can help you."

His words were music to my ears, even in this fugue state, when I hardly knew who I was and where I was located. "Then, tell me what to do."

"This will take a commitment on your part."

"Yes, I'll do anything, so long as it doesn't harm my family, Elizabeth, or Jakjak."

He waited for moment, formulating what he wanted to tell me, in highly-exacting terms: "Dr. James...You are, unfortunately, a *link*. Quite possibly the best link we have."

"You mean Omar."

He nodded slowly. "Omar. More or less. There are other targets, but Omar must be stopped. Help us get Omar, and all of this will stop." He swept his hand in a wide arc and I was made to understand that he meant the nightmare that had become my life. "You see, Doctor James, in spite of what the public believes, there are many communications networks that cannot be penetrated. Even

The Encryption Game

with the world's largest super computers, you still can't get past the encryption. That is—unless you can get some piece of hardware or information from the enemy. And because you are the only real link to Omar, you represent to us the best possible chance for success in that area, I assure you. We have to have human intel. The encryption of our enemies cannot be broken, certainly not through interception. But if we get something at either end, some kind of key, some kind of opening, from either the sender or receiver, then..."

"I am not *linked* to Omar. Omar's a psychopath who has somehow determined that I'm a kind of hunting trophy. He's got a revenge complex."

"Indeed he does. And he will try to kill you again. For pride. And that is our link." He seemed to think for a moment, then said, "But there is another problem."

Again he waited, thinking his words over.

"The CIA, FBI, NSA—all of these agencies—are comprised of two groups: those who are bull headed enough to get every piece of evidence to prove the truth, and a small but significant number who'll play the politics of any event to stay on the good side of people from whom they may need a favor, or a promotion. Because that is the truth of the matter, the less the public knows about your activities, the better. You have to promise me, your savior and friend, that you will never take credit for your activities."

I was confused. "You know the man I killed was a terrorist, don't you?"

"I can help you. But I need you to watch your tongue. You cannot go rogue to the media, or anything like that."

"I have to defend myself."

He dropped his joint to the floor and stamped it out. "Just remember, the more you help us, the more we help you. We must penetrate his encryption. Help us get to Omar, and we can move mountains for you."

He walked to the door, rapped on the window twice, and turned and looked at me. "We've kept you in the loop, and we've kept you alive, because we know you."

"Everybody knows about me."

He looked at me like he knew everything I'd ever done in my life. The cell door slid open. He smiled as he slipped through the opening. "Not like we do."

Chapter 8

Virginia Peninsula Regional Jail
10:25 a.m.

I SAT IN THE back of the van as they transported me to my court appearance at the federal building in Newport News. As soon as we pulled out of the garage, the circus began. I could see through the tiny square windows of the van that the streets were lined with people

At first it was just a scattering, but as we neared the courthouse, the roads were nearly blocked. It seemed like half of these people carried signs. A few were professionally printed but most were crude and homemade. The nature of these surprised me. I'd expected signs saying something about me being a "Killer Doctor." The newspapers and the Internet had labeled me "The Syrian Refugee Killer."

But these signs weren't like that at all. They were mostly congratulatory. They were *congratulating me* for killing a Muslim refugee! "Kill all the Muslims," "Get Rid of More Refugees," "Good Man, Doc. Now Kill the Rest of Them," "Damn the Muslims," and others with similar messages. These people obviously believed every word that the media was saying about me.

With the national presidential election only a year away, many of these signs proposed me as a presidential candidate. But the most highly-visible of these political messages encouraged the election of Donald Bogart, the prominent Republican candidate who wanted to ban all illegal aliens and future Muslim applicants from ever becoming citizens. There were lots of signs saying "Bogart and James for President/Vice President."

The crowds were packed so densely at the entrance to the courthouse garage that we had to wait a moment for the police to move them aside.

Inside, I was lead through the halls by two U.S. Marshals. I wore a dark blue prison jumpsuit that had a wide restraining band around the waist. A chain ran from this restraint to my handcuffs, with a second chain running to the shackles at my ankles. Most people would have felt shame in this situation, but I held my head high, knowing I had protected our President. I wasn't guilty. I'd done the right thing.

We entered the stuffy courtroom through the back door. The judge, The Honorable C.R. Michaels, was an attractive elderly woman with her gray and black hair cut very short, and with half-rimmed glasses that seemed permanently stuck to her nose. A wide variety of people thronged the seats on the far side of the wooden partition where the U.S. Marshals sat me. I knew none of them, but suspected that they were mainly press, with a few tourist-types who'd secured their seat by waiting in line.

The courtroom procedure was short. I stood in front of the judge, with an officer of the court behind me, as the bailiff and the prosecutor spoke to each other in an obligatory exchange. Then the prosecutor read the affidavit demonstrating that the government had probable cause to charge me with a crime. For my actions in less than half a minute at the scene, there was a ten-minute listing of the facts surrounding the shooting — according to the way the government saw it. "Special Agent Hopkins then saw James take the rifle, aim the rifle specifically at Johnson, and fire a single shot. First responders at the scene pronounced Mr. Johnson dead roughly twenty minutes later, at approximately 5:45 pm, local time."

I was relieved when the reading finally ceased.

Following the reading of the affidavit, the judge asked me if I had a lawyer, to which I answered, "Yes." She then informed me that I would return in four days for an arraignment. No bail was set, and I was remanded back to the Virginia Peninsula Regional Jail, from whence I'd come.

Chapter 9

Halifax Avenue
Quantico, Virginia
11:00 a.m.

ELIZABETH KEYES WAS A rocket, thinly disguised as a good-looking woman. She carried in her eyes a look of laser-like focus. Beautiful, lustrous blond hair adorned her face, usually, although on this day she wore it up, piled high on her head. She had a great sense of style and she favored high-heeled, black leather boots that made her seem tall, although in reality she was of medium height, at five-feet-six.

Keyes had known almost nothing but the underworld for her entire life. Though she was an American, she'd grown up in London, in the home of foster parents, and had left at a young age. After leaving, she'd been a prostitute, and later, an assassin.

She'd been picked out of a brothel by the Jordanian Mukhabarat, the ruthless secret police who'd used her to get into the bedrooms of world leaders and businessmen. The Jordanians had worked hard to erase all documents concerning her existence—birth certificates, grade school records, all of it.

Her first job had been to kill a Turkish Member of Parliament. She had injected an enormous amount of strychnine into his ear canal while he slept, to make it appear as though he'd had a heart attack. Considering the unusual location of the needle hole, murder was never suspected

Her handlers knew she was a prodigy and so they sent her to the best people, including Vasily Alexeyov, the notorious Russian computer hacker. After that, she'd gone to other mentors, each one as malevolent as the last.

When she was twenty-five, she met a small, unlikable man, Omar Farok, who claimed to be a prince. Farok had managed to steal her away from the Jordanians and hide her in his underground network, which wasn't hard to do considering the fact that Elizabeth Keyes possessed no paper trail whatsoever. Omar had made it possible for her to receive more training and had even let her take on private assassination jobs and keep some of the money, which, over time, amounted to a small fortune.

Then she met Scott James and everything changed. Farok had arranged for her to work in Dr. James' office in order to get close to a target, a man Farok wanted dead. There was a problem, though. Scott James was the first decent man she'd ever met. That confused the matter greatly. He was warm and funny and he put you at ease immediately. He was immensely handsome, but without a trace of personal vanity. Other women respected him, and wanted him. But it was more. There was something about the man. He gave you hope, reassurance, without really consciously trying.

Keyes had defected. She'd left Farok and had devoted herself to Scott James. For this, Farok vowed, she would someday be captured, tortured, and killed.

Keyes was now the most important informant in the entire American intelligence community. She'd logged hundreds of hours in interviews with the best interrogators. She was a gold mine of information, a once-in-a-lifetime opportunity for the people in Washington. In the first week alone she'd given them enough intel to uncover an Al Qaeda cell operating in New York. But the assassination of Emmanuel Johnson in Williamsburg changed everything. Though she still had immunity and the ability to operate covertly, she maintained her anonymity and freedom by the slenderest of threads.

All of these factors played on her mind as she walked through the beautifully manicured neighborhood where Roy Perkins lived. She needed Perkins' help. She wanted to see the only man she'd ever loved, Scott James, freed, and the only person she'd ever really feared, Omar Farok, dead.

At Perkins' home, a stately Tudor accented by a tall fence and two large azalea bushes in full bloom, she buzzed the intercom. An elderly man in a tuxedo greeted Keyes at the door. "Madam Keyes, I presume. General Perkins is waiting for you," he said with a decidedly British accent.

He led her down a hallway adorned by elegant antique chairs and landscape paintings of the Hudson River School. They passed the dining room where an attractive middle-aged woman in a stiff, bouffant hairdo, sat at an old Chippendale table with chairs for twelve people. The lady sipped from a demitasse cup, glanced at Keyes, and raised her nose.

They passed several closed doors, further on, before the butler stopped at one and knocked. "Ms. Keyes to see you, Sir," he said. With that, he turned and walked away.

General Perkins opened the door and invited her in. She took a seat at one end of a sofa and he sat on the other end. Around them, on the walls, hung dozens of diplomas, certificates of awards, a plaque displaying dozens of military service ribbons, and photographs of important military, political, and NATO dignitaries.

"I'm sorry to trouble you, Sir..."

"Call me Roy."

"Yes Sir."

"And no titles in this room."

"Yes, Roy. I'm sorry to be a bother to you but..."

"No bother. You came to ask a favor and you'll repay that favor by working with me on my own problem."

Roy Perkins' problem was well known. He was a man fighting for his life. After thirty-five years of brilliance in the Air Force, everything was now a shambles. His indiscretion, his affair with a junior officer, had exploded in the media at roughly the same time as the shooting of Emmanuel Johnson. Worse, it had come out that he was loosely affiliated with Dr. Scott James.

Roy Perkins had started out, all those years ago, as a

pilot, but he'd only spent two years in an active squadron. His superiors had recognized in him a great talent for intelligence matters. He handled huge amounts of data well, and he spent long hours studying the briefs that came out of the Department of Defense. After just twenty-four months on active duty, he'd been sent to work at the Pentagon. Slowly but surely, he'd made himself into the go-to guy on matters of terrorism/counter-terrorism and insurgency/counter-insurgency.

Soon, he was a star. He kept showing up on the television at Congressional hearings and at high-level White House briefings. At 57, Roy Perkins was a household name now, with all the perks.

The perks included the fact that fame attracts the opposite sex. This became a larger and larger factor as time wore on. Roy Perkins was small in stature, quite bald, and over the years he had become more and more dependent on his glasses. He had a mind that clamped on to problems like a vice, but that had rarely brought admiration from the ladies. Not that he was desperate for attention. He'd married when he was young and that had always suited him. Now, however, he was in trouble.

Perkins had been Deputy Direct of National Intelligence up until just two weeks before, and in that position he'd worked with Elizabeth Keyes. He knew all about Keyes' special abilities, or as much as could be known. She was the most mysterious human being he'd ever encountered in all his years in the intelligence business. She seemed to have no end to secrets. Estimating her, figuring her out, was next to impossible. All except one thing: She had a blind love, and lust, for Scott James. That part was obvious.

At Perkins' mention of his "problem," he instinctively lowered his voice a little and said, "We're in an 'I'll scratch your back but you must scratch mine in return' situation."

Keyes sat up straight. "Yes, I've been here before. What might I do for —"

"For me? Elizabeth, I know I was wrong, accepting the advances of Lt. Moss, but it was she who took advantage of me," he said as he massaged his face with his hands. He took a deep breath and stated, "My work has always taken first place in my life, but there was a time in my life, the period of time when Scott James was asking for my assistance, when Lt. Moss suddenly thrust herself on me. She kept taking off her clothes and kissing me. I repelled all of her advances, except for that one time, when she had my clothes off and in the bed."

"You didn't have to play her—"

"Her game? Yes, and I happen to know that in your distant past in London, you played Moss' role in these games."

Elizabeth didn't hesitate in giving her reply, "Are you calling Lt. Moss a prostitute?"

"No, I'm not calling her a prostitute. I'm calling her an operative. Regardless of whatever she might be, I can tell you one thing: That night, when Scott was calling me, I came close, but I did not penetrate her. I didn't... I...I came to my senses in time to leave the office and immediately write a letter demanding she be transferred elsewhere."

"But she..."

"That's right. She went to the base hospital and showed bruises which I did not put on her—my only touches were..."

"Yes, your touches were sexual caresses."

"That's right. I admit that. But I swear to God I never hit her. Somebody else did that. Not me. And she filed sexual abuse charges against me that very night."

"And your own commander believed her over ...?"

"Over me. Yes, but more than that, she handed over documents which I've never had in my possession and she said I gave them to her. And they bought her story. So that's why I'm asking you rather than all these wonder kids in the CIA: Who put Moss in that position to seduce me and who instructed her in her game? Give me that information and I can solve my dilemma."

"Can't you ask the NSA to handle that?"

"No. I can't. I cannot appear to be attacking a victim, you know, a victim of..."

"Rape."

Perkins collapsed in a heap. "I would... *never...*"

Elizabeth relaxed for a moment. "Did you ever 'talk' to her on your computer?"

"Yes, on my private laptop."

Elizabeth fidgeted in her chair before giving her answer. "I can help, but only if you let me have your..."

"Yes, my laptop."

She nodded.

"You can have my laptop," he said, and then he slipped a piece of paper across the sofa. On it were the words "CIA, I help Scott James."

Keyes, who knew as well as the General that his private residence was probably bugged, didn't miss a beat. "I'll scratch your back, Roy. So sorry to hear that you've been falsely accused."

Chapter 10

Day 4
Yanggakdo Hotel
Pyongyang, North Korea
10:00 a.m.

OMAR FAROK HAD HEARD nothing for three days, nothing at all. He was angry as hell.

Finally, at 9:49 a.m. on the third day, the phone rang. "Be down in the lobby at 10:00," the voice on the other end said.

Omar emerged from the elevator at 10:00 a.m., followed by four, tall, muscular Congolese bodyguards, wearing white suits and black ties. Also with him was Jack Fisher, his military hardware guru.

It was Fisher who had suggested that Farok seek out the cooperation of the North Koreans. Fisher had been indicted for selling secrets to the Russians, had subsequently escaped the United States by crossing over into Mexico, and had then contacted Emir Farok. There were lots of things Jack Fisher could tell Omar if Omar promised to keep him well-hidden from the American authorities. It was a good match, win/win.

Fisher was a thin man with sandy hair, and was something of a dandy. He wore a light-weight seersucker sport coat and gray trousers, even though it was cold out. All of the Koreans he'd met with so far wore heavy, blue military dress coats. Farok, wanting to keep up his image as Middle Eastern royalty, wore a heavy white thobe, with his wool, maroon and white keffiyeh.

The entourage crossed the modest, white and brown-marble lobby, and were met by a somber colonel who stood with his hands at his side and spoke discreetly, in Korean, as a lieutenant translated: "You are invited to see a display of our newest armaments, and afterward we will discuss what, if any, agreement that can be reached. We are going to Tonghae. Our Supreme Leader demands that you bring no cameras or recording devices with you."

The lieutenant patted down the clothing of the visitors, then turned to the colonel and spoke briefly. The colonel gestured toward the door of the hotel and began walking briskly.

That seemed like a pretty good sign to Farok. "Tonghae" meant the big missile launching facility that the North Koreans had put so much money and effort into. They were always showing it off to every foreign general

The Encryption Game

or international player who came through town. The Iranian Foreign Minister, for example, was in Pyongyang all week on a state visit, and there was no doubt that at some point they would take him on a tour of Tonghae.

The thirty-minute drive to the military airfield was along a pockmarked, eight-lane highway that was virtually void of other cars. The quarter-mile-wide, muddy Taedong River that ran beside much of the road looked bone-chillingly cold. There were no fishermen on its banks and only three work boats puttering lazily downstream and headed to the outskirts of the city. Women could be seen pedaling along on bicycles, while others peddled supplies beside the river to black-suited men. The few people that walked on the sidewalks of the capitol city wore brightly colored, fashionable clothes. In the distance, people wearing heavy black coats could be seen plowing the fields behind reddish-brown oxen.

At the airfield, the state jet, Kim Tu Sop's personal 747, waited to take the foreign dignitaries to Tonghae. Farok saw the Supreme Leader in the flesh for the first time, standing out by the aircraft, surrounded by his generals. Not surprisingly, Kim Tu Sop appeared smaller in real life than he did on television. Next to him was a taller man wearing a beige suit without a necktie, and very thin-looking when compared to the fat North Korean leader. Omar took this man to be the Iranian Foreign Secretary.

After a half-hour wait, Farok watched as the Supreme Leader jovially ushered the Foreign Secretary up the steps to the 747. Shortly afterward, Farok was rudely informed that he would not be traveling in the state jet. The Supreme Leader had decided that Farok would be going to Tonghae in a rickety, fifty-year-old C-47, flying like a peasant in seats with no cushions. This, Farok somehow blamed on Jack Fisher, who had of course been the one to suggest working with the North Koreans in the first place. For the hour, Farok continually snapped at his travel companion.

Tonghae Missile Facility
North Korea
11:05 a.m.

FAROK AND FISHER WERE seated in the Tonghae launch control room, four rows behind Kim Tu Sop's private box in the front row. Each time the smiley faced Kim slapped the Iranian's shoulder and laughed like a child, Farok scowled. The North Korean Supreme Leader never even recognized Farok's presence. He was burned.

The control room was lined with row after row of long consoles, with TV monitors stationed at every three feet. The rocket scientists and invited observers sat at the monitors and it seemed as though the North Koreans were trying very hard to copy the look of NASA's control room in Houston.

Through the window, Farok could see the North Korean's long-range missile, the newer version of the KN-14, one that could easily handle the needs of his planned EMP. The missile stood ninety feet tall and was stark white, with red lettering and a red nose cone.

But Farok was having a difficult time watching the

The Encryption Game

missile launch. Everyone in the control room was silent, or nearly so, and intent on observing the progression of the operation, all except Kim Tu Sop and his entourage. They were noisy, gleeful, and they talked on and on, loudly. This angered Farok even more. Omar sat with his arms crossed, in defiance of his inattentive host.

At last, the time had finally arrived. The count down proceeded from the one minute mark until it got down to the last few seconds. The room went silent except for a Korean woman's voice coming through a speaker overhead, counting the numbers: "Five. Four. Three. Two. One..." Flames gushed from the bottom of the slim white rocket. The ten-story tower, holding the missile, shuttered violently. Though the control room was a quarter-mile away, the noise was deafening. Farok placed his hands over his ears.

Kim Tu Sop screamed in glee. As the missile slowly lifted from the rocket baffle, Kim stood and applauded. The scientists and controllers in the room followed his lead, standing, clapping, and cheering wildly.

The rocket climbed two hundred feet into the air before angling downward, pointing its nose toward the East Korean Bay. Clouds of white smoke spewed toward the control center. Suddenly everyone ceased their applause, everyone except Kim Tu Sop. He broke from his entourage, still clapping, and ran outside to an observation deck. He watched the rocket speed toward the sea, maintaining an altitude of half a mile. It flew less than three miles from the launch pad before exploding in a huge ball of white smoke and falling into the bay.

Kim Tu Sop's face turned red. He started barking

orders. A four-man security team escorted Farok and Fisher to a black vehicle and headed back to the airport. Through the rear window, Farok observed Kim Tu Sop summoning a group of his scientists to his side. He reached up and grabbed a balloon-topped hat off of one of the military officers and started whipping the chief rocket scientist with it.

For the first time since they'd come to North Korea, Fisher saw Farok smile. "Good show," he said.

Chapter 11

Visitor's Partition
Virginia Peninsula Regional Jail
11:17 a.m.

I WAS HAPPY TO receive my first visitor, Elizabeth Keyes.

I walked into the visitation area and saw her sitting on the other side of the Plexiglass. I wanted to burst through the restraining wall and hold her in my arms. The best I could do was touch the glass that separated our hands.

She seated herself in front of the telephone and tried to say, "Scott, I..." but her voice cracked and a single tear slid down her cheek. I was a pathetic-looking prisoner in a prison jumpsuit, not at all the accomplished surgeon I had once been. Moreover, she knew I was innocent.

"I figured they'd have you in the slammer, too," I said.

"Me?" She shook her head subtly, knowing that she was being recorded, and probably filmed. "No, I'm covered," she said.

I nodded in understanding. "They mentioned your name at the hearing."

"What?!"

"They called you an 'undercover government informant, here called Jane Doe.'"

"That's not funny."

"Sorry, Janey."

"I think somebody wanted to bring me up on accessory charges, but the Feds said no way, Jose. Apparently I'm still too important to them. But I have a feeling that the matter may not be over."

"What *is* your name, exactly."

"Roxanne Kowalski."

"Why'd you pick that?"

"I didn't," she said, ruefully. The slight movement of her head told me "don't go there."

In the five minutes they allowed for her visit, she told me my two kids were fine and that she was working to get me out. I wanted some time to talk to her alone, but so long as I was behind bars, there would always be ears listening to our every conversation. I asked her if she thought I might get out on bail and she said, "The bail will be high, but you have the resources to cover it. I have talked to the lawyer's office and they're sending someone over today, a guy named Josh Edwards."

Our five minutes were up too quickly. I kissed the glass in front of her face and she did the same.

The Encryption Game

Her last words were, "When you're out on bail, we'll sort this all out."

Visitor's Partition
Virginia Peninsula Regional Jail
11:41 a.m.

ALMOST AS SOON AS I returned to my cell, I was informed that my lawyer was waiting for me. All three conference rooms at the tiny jail were taken, so I met him at the partition.

It was stuffy and hot in the confined little room where all the inmates sat, sweating, talking to visitors on phones. We were forced to talk through the glass.

Josh Edwards was young, about thirty, with a shaved head and a four-day beard growth which was obviously manicured each day to keep it at that state. He wore a Harris Tweed coat with preppy orange and brown squares, and a heavily starched shirt with a solid orange tie. He sat on the front edge of his chair and leaned forward, his face nearly touching the Plexiglass barrier between us. I could tell by his tense facial expression that he wanted to jump on my case and run with it. That was a good sign.

He had a list of questions for me about my background and what happened in Williamsburg when I shot Emmanuel. I had no secrets to keep from him so I answered truthfully, expanding some of my answers to give even greater detail. He wrote on his legal pad as fast as he could.

He then told me that the US Attorney General had declared jurisdiction over my trial because the killing of a foreign national under the protection of the US

Government constituted capital murder. I responded by saying that there was a small problem with that: The man I killed wasn't a foreign national; he was an American.

At the arraignment, in four days, Josh would accompany me. There, the judge would decide if I would be let out on bail.

Josh told me, "If you agree, I'll request a speedy trial, which will mandate that the trial be within seventy-five days."

I nodded. "It's urgent that I have some freedom to help in my defense. The case will be railroaded if I can't work with Elizabeth Keyes and find out what really happened. I'm guilty of killing Emmanuel. I killed him to prevent Omar Farok from killing our President. Get me a little space and I'll prove I'm not a cold-blooded killer but a patriot. I prevented the assassination of our President."

"Okay. Okay. Just take it easy. Ms. Keyes called me today. She said you needed photographs of the man you killed along with any videos made of the shooting. She sent me a very complex list of items she wants, fifty-three of them. We won't be able to address any of these until we get to Discovery."

"Discovery?"

"The prosecution is mandated to supply any evidence that they have pertaining to your trial. That's Discovery. In civil proceedings, the prosecution can drag their feet for weeks or months and withhold evidence until the last minute. That hampers the defense's preparation of a case. But in a case like this they can't dick around with the evidence like that. I've already made a court filing of Keyes' Discovery list. She seems pretty sharp."

The Encryption Game

"She's more than sharp. I'll bet my life on the fact that with three weeks of preparation, she could take and pass your bar exam. She has more than a photographic memory. Her judgmental skills are keen as well. She audited classes at Oxford University in England, and was the highest ranking person in her class, until they discovered she hadn't even paid tuition and wasn't even enrolled."

"I respect that, and I'll use all her talents to benefit your case. The discovery process can be complicated. The prosecution has to show us everything they have. We can have our own experts analyze whatever they have, and we can also make a motion-to-suppress. In other words, we can have some of the stuff thrown out. The FBI has taken everything to their facility just down the way."

Their "facility" was of course the FBI crime lab at Quantico.

"I want to see a photograph of the man I killed," I said. "Was he wearing a bullet proof vest and is he still alive?"

"Okay. Okay. We'll get to that. There were a lot of camera-phones taking pictures and dozens of TV people shooting video."

"But, I *am* guilty of killing Emmanuel."

"I know, but once you declare guilt, you're immediately sentenced, without any discussion of why you did it, or if you saved the life of the President. Do you want to spend rest of your life in jail?"

"No."

"Then, listen to me. Your plea is Innocent. Period. And don't say anything in that courtroom to the contrary. Do you hear me?"

He looked me straight in the eyes until I answered, "Yes."

"One of the good things about Federal Court is that there is no death penalty, like the State of Virginia has. Your worse sentence is Life in Prison. But I'll work to free you completely."

He looked me again in the eye. "I'm your attorney. Don't do or say anything in that courtroom. I'm your voice. Just keep your mouth shut and let me do the talking, do you understand?"

I nodded "Yes."

I knew at this point that had he been at my side he would have shaken or slapped me. He shouted, "Look at me and say 'Yes,' 'Yes' like you mean it! You have the reputation of making your own decisions, not relying on anyone else's advice, and going off on tangents, and getting yourself in more hot water than is necessary. I am your lawyer. You know nothing about legal matters. You're constantly in trouble, in part of your own making."

At first, I looked down. Even my own lawyer saw me as the fugitive I'd become.

I jumped as he slapped the glass wall between us and frowned. I looked up, intently in his eyes, and said with what little sincerity as I could muster, "Yes."

Chapter 12

Day 6
United States Courthouse
Newport News, Virginia
9:00 a.m.

MY "FRIENDS" AGAIN THRONGED the courthouse. They surrounded the entrance to the garage so tightly that the van couldn't get through. I could see them pressing up against the tiny window, trying to get a look at me. Inside the van, up front, I could hear one of the Marshals yelling to the local police, "Get these people back! Get out of the way! Get them back!"

The van crawled through the poster-waving fanatics until it got to the garage door and then we had to wait for the partition to slowly lift.

They again brought me in the back door, wearing the jumpsuit and chains. This time, however, the Marshals took me to sit beside my lawyer, Josh Edwards.

I was happy to see Elizabeth, out of the corner of my eye, sitting in a packed room of viewers.

There was not a moment lost in the courtroom. Josh touched my arm and said out of the side of his mouth, "Stand."

We stood and the bailiff read the case number and the charge of Capital Murder. As soon as he had finished, Judge Michaels immediately spoke into her microphone. "Who is defense and prosecution?"

"Josh Edwards, Your Honor, representing Dr. James."

"Jack Valenti, representing the 6th District, Your Honor."

The judge looked at Josh over her half-rimmed glasses and asked, "Does the defendant understand the charges against him?"

"Yes, Your Honor. He does."

"And how does he plead?"

This was my moment. I drew in a breath and said in a loud, clear voice, "Innocent, Your Honor."

The judge and bailiff took a moment to enter the plea into the record, and then the judge looked at the prosecutor and asked, "And what is the recommendation for bond?"

The federal prosecutor, standing at the table on the other side of the aisle, said in a loud voice, "In view of the violent nature of this crime, we feel that the defendant is a threat to society and recommend that he remain incarcerated until the time of his trial."

The judge looked over her glasses at Josh. "Counsel?"

The Encryption Game

Josh said loudly, "We disagree, Your Honor. The defendant needs time to assist in his defense and this is impossible in a correctional facility."

"Your Honor," the prosecutor said. "We believe that the defendant is an extreme flight risk."

"Your Honor," Josh broke in, "we wish to call attention to the Character Reference Letter submitted to the court by General Roy Perkins which—"

"Your Honor—"

"Which states 'Dr. Scott James has cooperated with the CIA in tracking down terrorists in America.'"

"Your Honor," the prosecutor said, "General Perkins is himself under indictment for criminal misconduct, including sexual assault. We ask that the court take this into consideration and deny bond."

I whispered to Josh, "Uh oh, this is bad."

"Your Honor," Josh started, "Dr. James has assisted in the pursuit and capture of numerous terrorists. If he is returned to jail he will be at great risk of personal harm. We request that the defendant be placed under the protection of the Department of Justice. This would eliminate any perceived flight risk."

The judge seemed to be mulling over the situation. Then she said quietly, almost as though it was an after thought, "Bond will be set at one hundred thousand dollars."

The prosecutor jumped up and said, "Your Honor! Common thieves pay more bail than that! If awarded at all, we ask the court for four million dollars bond."

The judge shot back: "Prosecution will calm down!"

"Sorry, Your Honor."

"The defendant will be placed under the protective custody of The Justice Department upon posting bond."

Josh reached over and patted me gently on the back. "We just got lucky."

Chapter 13

Farok's Office
Aden, Yemen
10:30 p.m.

JACK FISHER STOOD AT an architect's drawing table, looking over a diagram of the eastern half of the United States. Farok paced behind him, balling up both of his fists and rhythmically squeezing them as his face became progressively more red.

"Son of a bitch!" Farok screamed. "I was counting on your friends in North Korea, the ones you praised so highly. Their rockets are of propaganda value only! They all go parallel to the ground when they're supposed to go up in the air! And then they just go *puff!*"

"Yes, I know, but if you had the patience to wait a few

months..."

Farok waved his hands over his head and shouted, "Wait, wait, wait. That's all you have to advise me?"

"No, but—"

"Damn you!" Farok picked up a book from his desk and threw it across the room. "I buy the best experts and they lead me into a plan that is shit!"

"I'm on your side of this war."

"Sorry bastards! I can't fight my war without support. I trusted your words when I went to North Korea. I can only hope their bombs are better than their rockets."

"I can assure you on that. Every one of their bomb tests in the past five years has been successful. The bombs are not large, a little less that two kilotons, but that is more than enough power to create the destruction you desire."

Farok took a deep breath and clasped his hands behind his back. "That does me no good whatsoever if I don't have a rocket to get a bomb up to the altitude necessary for an EMP. If we set off the bomb at ground level, this does nothing. It destroys too much. I can't launch my raid. I can't—"

"There may be another way."

"Another way?"

Fisher thought for a moment, then said, "Send it up by balloon."

"Balloon?"

"Yes, a high-altitude balloon."

Farok's face turned red. "This is just more of your bullshit!" he shouted. "This is stupid! A balloon. Ha!"

"A high-altitude balloon could carry the bomb. I know a guy in Sweden who's working on just such a balloon.

He's a greedy little freak and he hates America. I know for a fact that he has a prototype that's ready for launch. For the right price, he could be bought."

"The world will laugh at this. The North Koreans will never go for it."

"On the contrary, Great Emir. This may be the reason why they've made no offer of a bomb. Think about it: They could go along with your plan to disguise the origin of the bomb, but a missile would be harder to disguise. A missile is a huge object. Smuggling it into the United States would be exceedingly difficult. But a balloon—nobody would be expecting that."

"Maybe."

"With the two kiloton bomb, I calculate that the E1 pulse we need can be created at eighteen miles altitude. This balloon that I'm talking about—it's designed to reach that altitude. And the blast will create fifty thousand volts per meter and will burn out most of the electrical circuits from Nova Scotia to the panhandle of Florida. Everything will be fried, from America's massive power grids to most of the cellular telephones. America will be crippled. All radio and television broadcasting will be irreparably destroyed. Your men are well trained and will be underground when the bomb is detonated. It can work."

Farok began to nod his head. "So, my plan to have my men underground when the bomb explodes will ensure my success?"

"Well...yes."

Farok balled his fists again. "Why do you hesitate?"

"We still have to get the bomb. And the balloon."

Farok took deep breaths. "I will contact the North

Koreans."

"You will be applauded as the world's hero."
"I already am applauded as the world's hero."
"Of course, Great Emir."

Chapter 14

Virginia Peninsula Regional Jail
Noon

IT WAS TIME TO go. I was being released. I was incredibly relieved—until I stepped out of the glass doors of the municipal building.

Suddenly it was like I was drowning in people trying to touch me. Cameras and microphones were thrust in my face. Questions began flying all around. Then, just as suddenly, a space opened up around me and all the cameras formed a haphazard organization, oriented toward one person, who was standing to interview me. The Marshals stepped aside as my interviewer stepped toward me and extended his hand.

"Hello, I'm Donald Bogart, and I'm running for

President, I want to congratulate you for your service to America in trying to keep the Muslim, Syrian Refugees out of our country." Under his red baseball cap with the message "Make America Strong Again," I saw the red coloration of his hair, matching a ruddy, Irish-looking complexion. I looked into his steel gray eyes. "When I am elected President, I will ban these people from our country, export all those here illegally, and prevent any more of them from entering our borders."

He stepped beside me, hugged my shoulders, and said, "May God Bless America," as the cameras rolled. Then, as quickly as he came, he disappeared into the crowd, and the mass of people converged on me once again. One television reporter shot a question at me while her cameraman all but blocked my way to the waiting car. "Are you happy about killing a refugee?"

"He wasn't a refugee. He was a terrorist."

"So you believe that all refugees are terrorists."

"What? No! Eh..."

Suddenly they were all throwing questions at me while Josh was pulling my arm, trying to get me to the car.

"Was making a single sniper shot part of living out your JFK-Lee Harvey Oswald fantasy?"

"What? No! I don't have any fantasies about—"

"What do you think we should do about the terrorist problem, Dr. James?"

"Simple. The Muslim clerics need to come out against it and that needs to be supported by Muslims and non-Muslims everywhere—"

"So you're very critical of Muslim clerics—"

"No! What?"

"Dr. James: Would you assassinate a refugee again if you had the chance?"

"What are you talking about? You're twisting everything around here—"

"So you're very critical of the media and Muslim clerics—"

"What? No! I don't mean that at all."

"Scott!" Josh whispered in my ear, "Just get in the car. Just get in the car!"

The tall newswoman pushed closer in: "So you believe that all the refugees work for ISIS—"

"No! There are other circumstances that have to be take into—"

"So you're a supporter of Donald Bogart."

"Well ... I ... Eh—"

"SCOTT! GET—IN—THE—*CAR!!*"

I felt a hand come down on my scalp and push me into the waiting limo.

Well, I thought to myself, *if they didn't hate me before, now they will*.

Cadet Dorm
FBI Training Center
Quantico, Virginia
1:10 p.m.

I WAS TRANSPORTED BY two FBI agents to the agency's well-known facility inside the Marine Corps Base in Quantico.

They handed me over to Special Agent Jane Hopkins, a person I vaguely knew. My life as an informant, or as I liked to say, an unwilling pawn, had put me in touch with many people like her.

Special Agent Hopkins was slightly tall and quite attractive, but she seemed determined to make herself into a frump. She had no sense of humor whatsoever. She had screwed up her hair at the top of her head into the tightest bun anyone had ever seen, and refused to smile at anything, under any circumstances. Nevertheless, she was now my "minder."

The furnishings of my captivity were spartan, with a frayed but cushy sofa in the front room, flanked by rickety side chairs that didn't match, either in style or color. The beds in the two bedrooms were metal-framed and rusty, like I'd only seen before in old movies. There was a single, wooden folding chair in the bedrooms, with a cheap but rather modern looking writing desk in each. Badly chipped black and white tile covered the floors in the kitchen and bathroom. There was rust in the toilet water and in the faucets in the bath and kitchen sinks. They called Quantico a classy place, but my take on it was that one of the many people in the world who hated me chose this apartment to further punish me.

Elizabeth was there and it was great to see her. We stood alone in my room for a moment, and then a look came over her face. "Scott," she said, reaching out to touch my arm, "don't worry about the press."

"I'm not."

"What's wrong?"

"My bail was too easy."

"What?"

"And there's something else, too. A guy came to my cell the day after my interrogation."

The Encryption Game

"What guy?"

"I have no idea," I said, shaking my head. "He was a tall blond guy I've never seen. He was smoking dope."

"What? Who was he with?"

"He wouldn't tell me. When I asked him if he was CIA, he just laughed."

"They always do. If you ask a CIA guy if he's CIA, he just smiles at you. They have a certain way of smiling, too, you can't miss it."

"No. This was different. He wasn't CIA. Regardless, he said he's a friend and he's watching me. He was *really weird*. I think he had a hand in getting me out, but I'm not sure about anything right now."

"You've got a bigger problem than that right now, Scott."

We sat side by side at the table as Elizabeth put five days' worth of newspapers on the table and began turning the pages. She pointed to one grainy newspaper photo after another, calling attention to the man I was accused of killing. In the pictures, he was in the front row of the cluster of refugees.

My voice was shaking as I looked at her. "That's not the man I killed!"

"There are dozens of photos of the man, Malcolm Johnson. Some of them are from the evening the President spoke."

"Why do they keep calling this guy 'Malcolm'? And why do they keep calling him a foreign national?"

She read slowly, "Malcolm Johnson, who was being considered by the Nobel Prize Committee for..."

"What is this?"

"There's something else. Look."

In the foreground of one shot, there was another man in the group standing near the President's podium. He was also tall and black, but in the picture, his face wasn't clear. He wore something thick beneath his shirt. "That may not be a suicide vest. That may be a bullet proof vest."

She said quietly, "This might not hold up in court, Scott, but I want you to know that it proves to the two of us that you did the proper thing in shooting him. That's Emmanuel, and we both know that he's Farok's man."

As we sat there, the reports on the man I was accused of shooting started rolling on her computer:

Reuters: Killed in Williamsburg, Va. Malcolm Johnson, humanitarian from the Congo, a well-known spokesperson for the Syrian Refugees, spent the past four months visiting European nations trying to get pledges of support for admitting refugees to their country...

Associated press: The US embarrassed. A much loved and highly regarded African killed in its Colonial Capitol...

Deutsche Presse: A man who convinced German Parliament to accept the refugees, killed by a mad man in America...

I interrupted. "That is not the man I shot. And as far as I know, he wasn't from the Congo, either."

I felt my heart fall to my feet.

"So, the world thinks I'm a mad man."

The Encryption Game

Cadet Dorm
FBI Training Center
Quantico, Virginia
4:10 p.m.

THE ONLY THING THAT saved me from total despair that first night was the arrival of my kids, Scotty and Jeremy, and my mother-in-law, Mrs. Hampton, whom I affectionately now called "Mom." Despite my divorce from her daughter, she'd stood by me. I'd expected that my former wife, Alicia, would have sought custody of the boys, but to the contrary, all Alicia sought in a companion was wealth. Love, like I gave her, meant nothing. Money was everything.

The boys and I romped and roamed all over the dorm. Mom smiled as she enjoyed our togetherness and being with "her three boys," as she called us. We were all worn out by 10:00 p.m., when Mom rounded up Scotty and Jeremy and took them down the hall to their room.

It was disturbing that my kids required protection, but this was my life now. More and more, the world saw me as linked to Omar Farok. Until that ended, I would have to endure.

With that mind, I took Elizabeth aside and told her the rest of what the man who had come to my cell had said.

"He said he wants me to try to get some kind of hardware from Farok, a laptop, a drive, or maybe a cell phone. That's all he really said."

"It's the encryption problem. It's getting bad. No one, not even the NSA, can break it when it's done right. They call it 'PGP,' 'Pretty Good Protection,' It's based on a mathematical formula that produces an almost infinite number of possible answers. It makes winning the lottery look like a good bet. It's impenetrable. If PGP encryption is done right, it can't be overcome."

"Of course it can. They've been doing it for years. Look at Edward Snowden."

"Scott, you need to learn about encryption. If people would bother to examine the Snowden leaks, they would see that the NSA couldn't decipher the messages themselves. All they could do was identify who was sending the messages and from what location. All they could do was identify who was calling whom, and for how long, that sort of thing. But they couldn't get the details. Modern encryption can't be broken."

"But they broke through the encryption of the iPhone of the terrorists in San Bernardino."

"No, they didn't. They figured out the guy's cell phone password. They put a program in the phone that allowed them to guess at possible passwords. You can guess at a password every eighty milliseconds, under normal standards."

"But it'll block you after a few guesses—"

"A good program can block the block. They can guess at millions of passwords if they've got the right software. It's the 'brute force' method."

"But they intercept cell phone calls all the time."

"That was the old days, Scott, like in the 90s, when not every link in the chain was encrypted. Now they use 'end-to-end' encryption. It's all impenetrable."

"Can't they—"

"Somebody's got to make a mistake. That's the

only way in." She looked at me gravely. "There was a faction...of my friends..."

"Your 'friends'..."

The use of the word "friends" was, itself, code. "Friends" meant Anonymous, the international hacker group. Keyes was unwilling to talk to me about only one part of her mysterious past, and that of course was her involvement in Anonymous.

She said, "This faction was called 'LulzSec.' Whenever they would hack, they would use a service called 'Tor,' which is a server that hides your location. When you use Tor, the NSA or whoever can't find out where you are. My friends worked from within Tor hundreds of times, and then one day one of LulzSec's hackers logged in to a chat room, but he forgot to go through Tor first. *Boom.* They got'em. Somebody made a mistake.

"But it goes farther than that. In the first place, ISIS and Al Qaeda say in their propaganda that they firmly believe that Pretty Good Protection can be broken. So they use multi-layered systems. They put the message in Excel, then they put it through Microsoft's Password Protect, which is unbreakable if you use a complex password, then they send it through end-to-end encrypted servers. And the messages contain poly-alphabetic cipher text, where any particular number can represent any letter in any part of the message—'1267' can mean the letter Q or it can mean the letter H. And they use code words like crazy. In Spy craft we call it 'nomenclature,' like they'll call a terrorist attack a 'wedding,' or a rocket launcher an 'eggplant'."

"But how do you figure it out? How do you the intelligence services get in and catch them?"

"Because terrorists make mistakes sometimes. In 2010, a British Airways employee named Rajib Karim tried to engineer an attack on a group of airliners. He put in layer after layer of encryption. But then he screwed up. He put the keys to the encryptions, the 'solutions,' plus what all of his code words and cipher symbols meant, on his laptop, under a file called 'Quran DVD Collection'. He figured that if he were caught, nobody would look there. They'd think that the file was just religious text. Well, he didn't fool anybody. He's in a British prison."

"He tried to hide in plain sight."

"It's called steganography. It's when you try to hide the *existence* of a message. Back in the Middle Ages they used to shave messenger's heads, write out the messages on their bald skin, and then they'd wait 'til the guy's hair grew back, then send him on his merry way."

I started laughing. "Now, *that*, I like. It's got a little style to it."

"During the Viet Nam War, an American POW was interviewed on international television. They asked him how he was being treated by the North Vietnamese. If he were honest, he would have said 'they're torturing us', but he would have been taken back by his captures and beaten and perhaps killed. So he said they were being humane. But if you watch the broadcast of this guy, he's blinking in a weird way. He's acting like he's tired and worn out, like he's losing it. But in reality, he's blinking Morse Code. He's spelling out, with his blinks, 'torture torture torture' over and over again."

"But people figure out that stuff in two seconds."

"Don't be so sure. It takes time. Time is always a factor

in encryption-decryption. The North Vietnamese didn't figure out the torture message until it was too late. The time obstacle in figuring out the encryption or the code is big."

I thought for a moment. "Maybe if I help the guy who came to my cell, he'll help me. If Farok were to make a mistake, maybe I could get something for this guy."

"Maybe."

"So how in the hell are you supposed to help Perkins? What does he want from you, besides access to your brainy 'friends'?"

"Believe me, he knows what I'm going to do. The only reason he's doesn't want to do it himself is because it would look like he's persecuting Moss. I'm going to do just what he'd do. I'm going to use a 0-Day."

She looked at me and waited.

"Okay, I'll bite. What in the hell is 'zero day'?"

"It's a virus that will get into her laptop when I send her a friendly email from Perkins' computer, like 'Happy Friday' or 'Cute Cat Video' or something like that. The virus will go in and monitor her computer and wait for her to decrypt a message from whomever it is she's working with. When that happens, I've got her."

"But if she's an operative, she'll be watching for that."

"Not if I do it right. Or she makes a mistake. Somebody's got to make a mistake. It's the only way in. Encryption, when done right, cannot be overcome."

I nodded. I waited for a moment, then touched her. She was ready for my interruption. Her kiss was so powerful I forgot where I was and all the years I might have to spend in prison. "You realize of course that they're listening to us," I said.

"I'm sure there are bugs and they're well hidden."

I nodded.

She pulled the clip from her hair and let it fall deliciously around her face, then began unbuttoning her shirt. She whispered, "People have been listening to me with men for years."

I'd seen her naked many times in the past, but her beauty continued to stop me. There was no way I could think about business. I softly ran my hands over her entire body, and kissed all the places my hands touched. She moaned quietly, then did explorations of her own.

"Come with me," she mouthed, and we went to the bathroom and I undressed, and stepped in the shower.

Making love in a shower is not as difficult as some people make it out to be, but talking after it's over is another thing. I was breathless.

The night was magical. My hands went all over her and she was all over me. It's not the sex that I'll always remember about that night, but the passion and the love I felt for her. I don't know how long we spent in bed, but when I awakened at 7:00, I looked at her face and felt warm all over. My mind was completely at peace.

Chapter 15

Day 7
Stockholm, Sweden
2:30 p.m.

THE FLIGHT WAS PROLONGED due to the need to avoid the air space over China and Russia. Jack Fisher spent the flight making phone calls and preparing for the mission ahead, while Farok slept.

The balloon designer, Sven Mobris, was a wealthy Swedish entrepreneur who owned his own factory in Stockholm. If a deal could be made, Farok's money would go far to finance the stratospheric projects Mobris had been involved in for the past ten years. His dream was to charter flights to the edge of space. Over two hundred people had already signed up and were waiting for the project to begin in 2019.

Mobris had an office just outside the airport property, where he was waiting for Farok. He answered the door in his red, yellow, and blue floral-patterned short sleeve shirt, orange shorts, and high topped black tennis shoes with no socks. His facial hair growth was at least five days. As Sven opened the door, Farok gasped. They stood toe to toe, both of equal height at five-six, with the portly Sven facing the pencil thin, debonair, Omar Farok. It took a moment for Farok to adjust to the sloppy appearance of the best balloon expert in the world.

After a short handshake, Sven bounced to his desk and laid down photographs of a recently finished balloon, one that had taken his shop eight months to produce. He was energized, not by any recent overload of caffeine but by a state of perpetual mania. "Jack told me what you need and this balloon exactly fits the bill."

The overall frenetic atmosphere created by Mobris made Farok take a step back. He slowly turned and looked at Fisher, and asked, aloud, "Is this guy stone fucking crazy?"

Sven screamed at these words. "Fuck you, camel jockey! You're the guy who wants to kill everybody in the world! And I'm the guy who's nuts? I don't need your fuckin' money! I'll have this balloon sold within the week!"

Mobris gathered up his plans and photographs and was putting them in his file cabinet when Fisher jerked Farok's arm and whispered in his ear, "Without the Korean missiles, this is the only way you can meet your deadline.

Now kiss and make up."

Farok made fists as he glared at the wall.

Sven walked to the door. "Show's over, assholes. Now get your asses out my door."

Fisher grabbed Mobris' arm and pulled the little mad guy to face Farok. "Sven, The Emir will buy your balloon, and he has the money ready to pay you."

Sven shook his head and turned away. "Not for sale."

Fisher countered, "I know you. You'd sell your own kids for the right price."

Farok managed a smile. "I'm sorry I was...rude. I have the $250,000 cash here in this case."

"Price just went up. It'll cost you twenty million. And the price is not negotiable."

Farok's face flushed. He took a deep breath, but Fisher answered for him. "Sold."

Farok quickly added, "I need the balloon ready for a launch next Thursday."

Sven took a step toward Farok and squinted his eyes. "I can make that deadline, for an extra ten million."

Farok again balled his fists but Fisher intervened. "That's fine. Take the $250,000 and we'll have the rest for you next Thursday, payable on lift off."

A smile crept over Sven's face. "Thirty million over regular purchase price. I can live with that."

Fisher shook hands with Sven as Farok stormed out the door.

Chapter 16

The US Attorney General's Office
Washington, D.C.
4:41 p.m.

A CALL CAME ON Eric Garret's private line. He sat, reading the papers on his lap and running his fingers through his long, black hair. At sixty years old, Garret was strangely youthful-looking, with almost wrinkle-free facial skin. After a moment, his secretary spoke: "Sir, after being up all night, I know you don't want to be bothered again by the terrorist case in Williamsburg, but you've received a request for Discovery. The Deputy Attorney General thinks you need to see this."

He stood, yawned, and stretched his small, thin body. "I'll be in at 7:00 tomorrow. Set up the appointment then." He walked to the full-length mirror hanging on his private bathroom door and adjusted his crimson tie, which displayed a small Harvard shield at the bottom. "Call Jim Tesh if there's a problem. He'll know how to reach me."

He was opening the rear door to exit when his secretary spoke again. "But, sir, it's Deputy Tesh who's here and requesting your audience."

"Damn," he said. He closed the door, walked back to the entrance of his office and saw Deputy Tesh standing there, cradling a file against his chest and waving in two other deputies.

Garret watched the others pull up cushy, crimson red covered side chairs and position themselves before he took his seat. "You fellows were up all night with me on this same case, so you know how I feel. Let's get on with it."

Tesh placed three pages of paper on his desk, all filled top to bottom with the requests for Discovery.

Garret picked up the pages, and went through the items, one by one, before tossing them back on the desk. "This Doctor James has one helluva lawyer to compile such a list."

"He's getting help from James' girl friend, Elizabeth Keyes."

"Who is this woman, Elizabeth Keyes? Is she Harvard trained?"

The deputies all looked at one another before Tesh spoke. "She's no lawyer. In fact, we can't find a record of her ever going to school anywhere."

Garret picked up a page of her Discovery requests and pointed to an item. "How would an untrained lawyer know to ask for 'Unedited and unadulterated video from post cameras, six through twelve, from the Capitol Building roof from 4:50 to 5:18 on the day of the defendant's infraction'? Or this one, 'The names of the eleven Secret Service Officers near the podium, the five on the second floor of the capitol building, and the three on the roof of the capitol building, along with the names of the two snipers on the roof.' It's been only seven days since the shooting and how many of you know the numbers and positions of the secret service members and the snipers, or even what a fucking 'post camera' is?"

Without waiting for an answer, he waved his arms in the air and shouted in his squeaky voice, "None of you! And not me, either! I want you and you and you," he pointed at his deputies as he talked, "to dig up some dirt on this Elizabeth Keyes. And be certain not to give her any information that will hamper my trial!"

Chapter 17

Day 9
FBI Crime Laboratory
Quantico, Virginia
10:21 a.m.

"I won't be able to get over there today," Josh said over the phone.

We were scheduled to go to see the videos taken on the day of the shooting. But now there was a slight hitch. "We still want to go," I said. "Besides, we know what we're looking at it."

"But you don't know what'll work in a court of law."

"That's true, but it wouldn't hurt just to let us look."

"No, it wouldn't. Okay, let me know if you see anything out of the ordinary, but I'll still have to go back with you later in the week."

Discovery had been somewhat clumsily arranged, or so it seemed to me. For one thing, the first item on the list, the photos taken of the victim, were still in the hands of the Prosecution. "What about the death photo?" I asked.

"Uh, yeah," Josh said. "I have a phone call in right now. Sometimes that happens. Just go over and look at the videos for today. We'll get everything they have, eventually."

Twenty minutes later, with the guidance of Agent Hopkins, we ventured over to the Crime Laboratory to look at the various video taken on the day of the shooting.

Inside, projection screens from two square feet to forty square feet hung on the surrounding walls, with rows of photographic instruments on long desks and comfortable, leather, swivel chairs for viewing.

A young Marine, introduced to us as Sergeant Willis, seemed to be the sole person working at the facility. He was all business and all military. He saluted as we walked in and then showed us to our seats before a four-by-four screen. He dimmed the lights and announced, "Camera 4307, placed by the Secret Service, 3:00 pm the day of the President's speech. I'll begin at 16:50 hours, that's ten minutes before the President's speech. The camera was placed on the roof top of the Colonial Capitol building, south side, direction 090 degrees, angle 032 degrees, field of view, 175 by 190 meters."

He started the film. It was typical surveillance video, grainy and without sound. The movements of the Syrians were restrained by the large crowd. Time was indicated in the upper right of the screen. The throng began to separate at 4:51, as the fifty Syrians were moved to the front of the gathering, within 120 feet of the podium. At 4:55, the group bunched together. At 4:57, the refugees looked intently at the podium.

"Stop the camera a second. I want to find Emmanuel." Sgt. Willis complied and I leaned close to the screen. The people were packed so tightly, it was difficult to see anything. Then, there was a black man who was a head taller than the Syrians.

I signaled Sgt. Willis to roll the film.

I could see that Emmanuel was turning his head. He moved to face the camera when a puff of smoke blurred the screen momentarily, then all I saw was the back of his head. Damn.

The projectionist moved the frames back to the spot I wanted. Again there was a momentary blur, which resembled some kind of smoke in front of the camera.

I shrugged. "What happened?"

"Looks like a cool blast of Arctic air hit the lens and caused water vapor. That happens sometimes this time of year."

The second film, from the Capitol roof, faced east. It was immediately to my left as I'd attended the President's speech. I watched a view of the crowd that was much the same angle as I'd seen on the day I shot Emmanuel. I watched the moving crowd, and its separation as the Syrians approached the stage. Then, at 5:00, I saw the tall black man. Something thick and heavily padded was under his clothing. My heart thundered in my chest as Emmanuel turned to the camera. But there was the sudden blur of his face. I saw that his hand dropped toward his pocket. This was the moment I chose to take my shot.

101

Then, his entire body jolted as I fired. I saw the explosion on his mid-sternum. He staggered, and dropped straight down. People crowded around and all I saw was their backs. They didn't run from the man I killed. Instead, they just crowded closer. All the camera showed was dozens of people hovering over Emmanuel's body.

I looked at Elizabeth. She frowned. I had Sgt. Willis go back over the scene, frame by frame. As the blur appeared on Emmanuel's face, I said, "Who marked up the film so we couldn't recognize the man's face?"

Willis stopped the film and went to the three frames that were blurred. He enlarged it, enhanced it, darkened it, and added more light, but the blur remained.

I stood and walked over to him. "Someone tampered with this film. Was it you?"

He was not intimidated. "No sir. I'm just the screen man. These came here in a box and I've shown them to three other people, and they've not changed since the first viewing. And, Sir!: I just do my job."

Elizabeth spoke. "Someone's messed with both of those films, the vapor theory doesn't work for me, and on this film someone has intentionally obscured Emmanuel's face."

Willis shook his head and looked at Elizabeth directly. "Nobody at this facility has done anything to change the film in any way. I'm the person who receives all the films we get here for analysis. I take 'em in, I lock them up, and I show them when authorized to do so. This goes for these films in particular and all the thousands of films that go through this institution. Hang your hat on that."

After a prolonged silence, I suggested we see all the other films. The first two had the better angle and showed more, even with the facial smudges, than did all the others. That was a big disappointment. Sgt. Willis went on to roll film of the aftermath of the shooting. After four minutes, the crowd began to disperse. I kept my eyes focused on the spot where I shot Emmanuel. The Syrians walked away from the area, but there was no body there. Instead, a body, covered with a sheet, lay five feet in front of the place I shot Emmanuel, and about six feet to the left.

"I didn't see anyone move the body there, did you?"

Elizabeth watched the film again. "I didn't see anyone move it, so how did it get so far away from where he was shot?"

Willis spoke, "Sir, it looks to me like there were a lot of people moving around at that time. Maybe you were mistaken as to where your shot ended up."

Elizabeth saw me bristling and interrupted, "How about television filming?"

"Their cameras weren't pointed in that direction. Same with the cell phone cameras in the audience. All the cameras were pointed away from the victim, and toward the President. No sir, they weren't trained on the area of your interest until after the shot was fired."

"Can the blurring of the face be corrected by your technicians?" I asked.

"No sir. These films are the final product."

"Are there other film sequences we can see?" Keyes asked.

"No ma'am. These are all we have."

He stood at attention, waiting further questions. We'd hit a brick wall. I turned to leave, but Elizabeth said the polite thing, which I refused to say, "Thank you."

Chapter 18

Unnamed Landing Strip
Pyongyang
North Korea
12:31 a.m.

FAROK, WEARING HIS SILK thobe and maroon keffiyeh, which covered most of his face, emerged from his private Lear jet 60, followed by his Congolese bodyguards in white suits and black ties. It was dark out, a condition made worse by the fact that there were no lights on anywhere at the small airport. Even more, the airport seemed to be in the middle of nowhere.

At the bottom of the stairs leading from the plane, Farok met a waiting military entourage which stood at attention. A somber colonel stood with his hands at his side and spoke loudly in Korean as a lieutenant translated. "Our Supreme Leader, and the people of North Korea, welcome you to enjoy the hospitality of this great and powerful nation."

To say that the situation was strange was quite an understatement. All the trappings of a state visit were apparent, but they were standing in the dark. The North Koreans seemed to be trying to show a little respect, for a change, but they obviously didn't want the prying eyes of the American satellites to identify who it was they were showing respect to.

The colonel spoke to Farok again: "Your men must remain in your aircraft while you accompany me to meet with The Minister of Security and Defense."

Farok nodded and walked with the colonel to a waiting Pyeonghua van, one of the very few, genuine, North Korean-made vehicles in the world. The two men stopped, and Omar got in the back with the colonel, while the interpreter got in front, beside the driver. The colonel sat rigidly erect and remained silent.

As the Pyeonghua wound its way through the capital, Farok took in the sights, the biggest one being the Ryugyong Hotel, a magnificent, ninety-five-story pyramid of light gray construction blocks which had been under construction for over thirty years. Financial difficulties had rendered it unfinished and unoccupied.

The car passed through the city and across the Taedong River to the Yanggakdo Hotel. The colonel, still silent, led them through the modest, white and brown marble lobby and to the elevator.

The Encryption Game

They exited on the fifth floor, and were greeted by the bright smile of a military officer with three gold stars on his collar patch. He reached to shake Omar's hand. "Welcome to The People's Democratic Republic of North Korea. Our Supreme leader sends his greetings. I am General Kyong Sun Som and I know you will share our Republic's appreciation for the art work that adorns our hallways." He gestured to the propaganda murals that covered the walls all the way down the long hallway. Though written in Korean, their messages were clear. The graphics showed soldiers as well as common people waving swords and guns at men with "USA" crudely written on their clothing. Several had civilians holding bombs with "USA" printed on them, and Korean children shooting at American civilians.

"So you see, we share your hatred of The Great Satan, USA, as you call it."

Omar remained stone faced as he looked at the murals along the halls.

The general entered a room halfway down the hall and directed Farok to a modern looking mahogany table in the middle of the room. A man with four stars on his collar was introduced as General Sang Bae Bok, Minister of Security and Defense. He rose and extended his hand. An interpreter translated from Korean to Farok's native Arabic: "Grand Emir Farok, The People's Democratic Republic of North Korea welcomes you. Our Supreme Leader will not be with us today, but he will observe our activities as we proceed." He pointed to a TV camera.

Emir Farok bowed and shook the hand. He sat on a straight-backed chair with a thin, Naugahyde cushion, across the table from the Korean general.

The general went straight to the business at hand. "Grand Emir, we wish as much as you to destroy our common enemy. We must admit, we are very impressed with your ingenious plan. Your deployment of a high-altitude balloon is something they would never expect. With your loyal ISIS following, we will work together to bring down America."

Emir Farok, who continuously twisted his long, thin, pasted-on and weaved mustache, nodded.

"We have our own nuclear warheads, enough to humble, but not enough to kill, the military giant. If we are identified with the action that you propose today, the USA will destroy our economy, much greater than they already have, and use their thousands of nuclear bombs to kill every one of our people. Our Supreme Leader will back you in your plan to bring harm to Satan in such a way as to permit your soldiers to overtake the military bases long enough to seize and transport their nuclear bombs to your Middle Eastern friends. With all that power, you will destabilize their powerful hold on the world. But we want your assurance that this is precisely what you intend to do. Do you swear this is so?"

Farok pointed to the ceiling. "I swear to Allah above and to the President of the People's Democratic Republic of North Korea that my plan will work."

"And do you swear you will maintain complete secrecy of Korea's supplying this package to you?"

Farok spoke loudly, "I swear complete secrecy."

The general followed. "Our long range missile systems are well developed, and other nations, even the United

States, considers them as good their own."

Emir Farok cleared his throat and shifted in his chair. He wanted to respond by saying that if this were the case, he wouldn't need Mobris' balloon, but knew that if he said something like that, it would be the end of the conversation.

The general continued: "We have the ability to destroy targets over the entirety of that enemy nation. It is unfortunate that sanctions imposed on us by America and her allies have delayed our acquisition of several parts for our rocket guidance system. But the alternate delivery system that you propose changes everything."

Farok looked at the camera. "I swear to The Supreme Commander that your nation will not be held responsible, and that I can deliver your weapon to the proper place so as to completely disrupt the USA's military activities for many weeks. And during that time, I will sell the nuclear warheads that I confiscate. The buyers have already made plans to quickly use the warheads to obliterate America's ability to control world events."

The previously blank monitor beside the camera lit up and displayed the face of North Korea's President. He spoke slowly and thoughtfully: "Your plan is pleasing to me. We are allies in our mutual goal. We will destroy your Great Satan."

"Thank you Supreme Commander."

The President then said, loudly, "I have a reputation of unmercifully slaughtering anyone, even my own friends and relatives, who betrays my confidence, so you know your fate if your mission fails. I have agents working all over the world, and they will find you if you do not do exactly as you have sworn here today to do."

Farok felt a rush of dread-filled adrenaline. He rubbed his mustache before answering. "I know of the kind and deliberate ways you are known for."

There was a long pause in the room. Farok spoke up, "Supreme Leader, I have a very tight timetable. I must have the, uh, the package, delivered within five days' time."

The Supreme Leader smirked. It was as though he thought Farok so naive as to be a child. "I assure you, Emir Farok, we've had a 'package' sitting on US soil for quite some time, waiting for the right opportunity to come along. You only need to go to the right place and you can pick it up like you are picking up a sack of rice at the market." The President's smirk grew to a wicked smile. "Use it wisely."

With that, the monitor went blank.

Chapter 19

Cadet Dorm
FBI Training Center
Quantico
2:00 p.m.

"SOMETHING'S NOT RIGHT."

"No kidding," she said. "Somebody tampered with that film."

"I haven't told you about my interest in the John F. Kennedy assassination."

"You don't need to. Half the country knows about it. Yes, I know about your thesis."

"The Italian Carcano 91/38 was the rifle attributed to the killing of JFK—"

"Scott... Scott... You shouldn't go into that. You

shouldn't even bring that up. It looks bad. People think that your obsession with the JFK assassination is one of the reasons why you took that shot."

"It's not an obsession. Just listen to me for a minute. I borrowed four different caliber rifles from gun shops, took them to a college acoustics lab, fired the Carcano, recorded the sound prints on tape, then, in a blind firing of all four, tried to learn which of the four was the Carcano."

"That's interesting, but that didn't prove anything. All you showed was that there wasn't an acoustic signature of the Carcano, or at least one that would set it apart from the others."

I smiled. You couldn't get anything past this woman with the photographic memory. "I'm not talking about proving anything. I'm pointing out the fact that there's more than one way to analyze this thing. Maybe all of the cameras were pointing the other way on the day I shot Emmanuel, but there will be many, many audio recordings out there. Many of them very close to the Emmanuel I killed. I want to hear them."

"Why?"

"Maybe there's something there."

"Or maybe they've been doctored."

"And I'll know if they've been doctored because I'll use an oscilloscope on them."

The Encryption Game

Cadet Dorm
FBI Training Center
Quantico
11:00 p.m.

"FAROK DEFINITELY BELIEVES HE'S been hacked," she said. "I've been talking to my friends. One of them was sent a message that they got from God-knows-where. It contains all kinds of code. He's putting in multiple layers of encryption in all his messages, something he's never done before. He's using a lot of cipher text."

"Cipher text?"

"Cipher text is where you substitute letters or symbols or numbers for the plain text letters. It looks like gibberish, but it's a message."

"And you know how to read it."

She smiled, seductively. "The Kama Sutra lists forty-three skills that a woman should possess, one of them is the ability to create 'secret writing,' what's known today as encryption."

"So every woman can be a spy?"

"No, so you can write steamy love letters and only your boyfriend will know what you're saying."

I could feel myself smiling. "See, now this is the reason I shouldn't trust you... among other things."

"You'd better trust me. I'm the only one in this world who believes your story right now."

"But isn't that the way they caught Mary, Queen of Scots—they deciphered a letter to one of her lovers."

"Well..."

"Mary was hacked."

"Very funny, Scott."

"Is it possible to decrypt Farok's message?"

"I'm working on that now. There are a couple of big variables in decryption. If the messages are 'single key' or 'symmetrical' decryptions—"

"What does 'single key' and 'symmetrical' mean?"

"That means that there is one key. It means that the guy on the other end has a chart that tells him what each of your symbols means. When they use that, it makes decryptions a lot easier."

"So what is there besides the 'single' key encryptions?"

"Well, there's the 'public key' or 'asymmetric encryption', where there are two formulas needed for decryption. One is used by the sender to encrypt the message and another is used by the receiver to *de*crypt the message. That's the basis for Pretty Good Protection, PGP."

I raised my eyebrows.

"Then there is the problem of just getting in, which usually means figuring out passwords. It's the other important variable in decryption: the length and complexity of the password. If it's eight or fewer characters, I have apps that will solve them, not instantly, but over a one-to-three-hour span. If somebody's using a word that can be found in a dictionary, like 'hacker' or 'Chicago,' then it's even easier. But when the password is random, and most especially, if there is a special character, like a percentage sign or an exclamation point, then the difficulty goes off the scale. We're talking billions of possibilities."

"That sounds difficult."

"It is. Like I told you before, it's impenetrable, if

done right. Even more, terrorists, and a lot of other people throughout the world, are now using WhatsApp, or Telegram, or Signal. They're messaging services that erase the message completely once it's been received. Even if you can get to their cell phones or computers, you still can't retrieve the data. Farok is using WhatsApp. He may be using another one, too."

Now I was really confused. My face must have betrayed that.

"I'm not sure what I can do with Farok's messaging. I won't be able to decipher the messages. But if I can locate the computers on the other end of the messages, I can put the times of sending and receiving together, like what the NSA does, and match them with the other computers of the people involved with them. That's one advantage you have when tracking someone using something like WhatApp. You can't tell what they're saying, and many times you can't retrieve the data, but most of the time you can know where they are. Knowing that may help you get a piece of hardware from Farok."

Chapter 20

Day 10
Airport Manager's Office
Elkins Regional Airport
Elkins, West Virginia
10:06 a.m.

LARRY WALTRIP'S PRIVATE LINE rang. He pushed aside the clutter of papers on his oversized desk and picked up. "Waltrip speaking."

Jack Fisher had talked to Waltrip before. He'd picked the Elkins Regional Airport for the launch of the balloon because of its location. The small airfield was tucked away from public view, but geographically close enough to Washington so that the balloon could easily drift into position with the prevailing winds. Fisher did not relish returning to the United States, where he might be picked up and sent to prison for selling secrets, but Omar had assured him that with a false identity he wouldn't have to worry. Farok's forgers could make a passport and driver's license that would pass all scrutiny.

Using his new alias, Fisher said, "Larry, this is Jack Phillips from World Aeronautics. We talked before."

"Oh, yes, Jack. Are you still interested in doing that trip to Front Royal?"

"Yes. I have a client who wants to test his equipment on that short flight. How's your schedule for next week? He wants to bring his equipment there and use it on Thursday morning. He'll require a hangar for all his equipment, and will be gone by noon, Thursday."

"This is a busy time for us. We're getting ready for an airshow the following week. There's a lot of servicing and repair work to be done on the runway." He thumbed through his flight manifests before saying, "I have four planes arriving Thursday afternoon that will need the hangar space, so if you can assure me that I will have my hangar back by three in the afternoon, it's a go. And, oh, I don't have any workers to assist your friend. Is he alright with that?"

"Yes. He has his own personnel. He only requires one of your runways on Thursday morning. Then he'll be gone."

"If he gives me the money the day he comes, in the form of a certified check, he can have Hangar D, as well as the runway until three o'clock."

"What's the total cost?"

Waltrip tapped out numbers on his pocket calculator and replied, "That package is $9,560.00."

"I assure you, the man providing the money is loaded.

The Encryption Game

I'll confirm for him."

"Have the check here before he brings in any of his stuff."

"I presume in that rural area there's no problem with burglars and such? My client will bring some sensitive research modules and doesn't want any rednecks roaming around and stealing anything."

"I have only one night watchman, but since I started this airport forty years ago, nuthin's been taken. It's totally safe."

"Only one night watchman, eh? Sounds perfect for our needs."

"What'ya mean by that?"

"Oh, nothing. Tell your watchman my client will have his own security, day and night, and we don't want anyone in that hangar checking on his new inventions. Nobody day or night."

"Not a problem. I won't even go over there. The space will be all his, with no interference from my people, and his secrets will be secure."

Chapter 21

Roy Perkins' Home
Quantico, Virginia
1:00 p.m.

THE BUTLER ESCORTED KEYES into Roy Perkins' office.

Perkins stood and extended his hand to her. After a cordial handshake, he asked, "Did you get it?"

"I have a lot more than what you asked for. Do you have something for me?"

He sat at his desk and rubbed his face with both hands before looking up. "That depends on what you offer in return."

Keyes had played this cat and mouse game many times in the past and had rarely come up the loser. "Give me what I want and I'll give you yours."

"Don't you trust me?"

"I know enough not to trust anyone in the intelligence community."

"Are we at an impasse?"

After a long silence, she finally said, with a quiet voice, "As they say in the South, 'I reckon so.'"

"Well, I'm certain a person of your intelligence has played the game of chess in the past, and I'll bet you can whip the ass of the top chess player in the world."

She remained mute.

"In a game of chess, they'd call this a stalemate."

She shook her head. "No. I have more cards in my deck than you have in yours. It might take time, and a couple court delays, but I have the ability to get my information from other sources. You don't. And with your Court Martial coming up, you're at the end of your rope. You'll hang for not having what I brought to you."

"I can have intelligence people still loyal to me at that door in a second and have them strip the information from your person, leaving you with nothing in return."

"You don't have to call out the Marines, I'll give it to you." She held the MacBook Air chest high. "Here, take it," she said, and gently placed the computer on his desk. He reached for the computer, then drew his hand back. He folded his arms. "What's the catch?"

"There's no one on earth who can decrypt what I brought you, not in a thousand years. I have to have something, anything, that will exonerate Scott James. If I like what you have, I'll release my material to you."

Sweat broke out on his face. Wet circles appeared on his chest and under his arms. The two stared each other. Keyes didn't blink.

The Encryption Game

"I have something you won't believe," Perkins said, and eased his hand to the corner of his desk.

She crossed her arms.

Perkins' hand touched a concealed button and slowly pressed it.

There was a commotion in the hall. The door opened and two men whom Keyes had never seen before approached the general.

Elizabeth sat with her back arched, half expecting the men to assault her.

They stood before the general and waited. Perkins nodded slightly and one of them handed a folder to Keyes. "This is what I surmise you came for," Perkins said. The two men, who were obviously intelligence operatives, nodded to Perkins and marched out the door. As they left, the butler entered with a silver tray bearing a steaming cup of coffee. He bowed slightly as he placed the coffee at a small end table by Keyes' chair.

Keyes opened the envelope and looked at the death photos of a man she'd never seen before. She looked up at Perkins. "That's not the right guy. Scott shot a different man. I need to know if..."

"Yes, Elizabeth. That's the person who was actually killed. Malcolm Johnson. A bona fide benefactor to society, so my sources tell me."

"But is he really...?"

"Dead? Yes. Look at the bullet hole centered in the man's chest. That's not a cigarette burn or some other effect. I don't know what kind of doctoring they're going to do to the picture they're going to show you, but this is real. No one else in the world has this photo. And from my vast experience in dealing with weapons, the gun that fired the bullet was not from the M-25 SWS sniper rifle Scott took from the sniper, but a standard .45 caliber pistol. Look at the size of the wound, the powder burns closely packed at the entry wound, and the depression around the wound." He thrust his index finger, touching the picture of the bullet hole. "That tells the real story. Not only was the gun close to the body, as the compacted powder burns reflect, but the pistol was pressed hard against the chest, leaving a rectangular imprint of the .45. It was shoved very hard against the man's chest when the trigger was pulled."

As she opened her mouth to speak, he cut her off by saying, "It was pressed against this man's body in an effort to suppress some of the noise of the gunshot."

"Why did ..."

"I'm not sure," Perkins said. "That's all I can do. I don't know the rest."

"Roy, I want to thank you."

"In my position, I've never yielded to pressure from a negotiating power. Let's just say, we made a diplomatic compromise." He dropped in his chair and put his head on his folded arms. When he looked up, tears covered his face. "This whole sexual assault matter has wrecked my psyche. My entire life is at stake. I don't mind losing my wife. She's been a royal bitch. It's the years of slaving over my job, the long days and nights I've studied and worked to get to the top. I'm there now, but that all will end with my conviction, the demotion to the lowest rank in the military, being imprisoned with murderers and rapists..."

He stood and approached like a child, begging forgiveness for one of the petty things kids do, his hands

The Encryption Game

folded in front of him like an altar boy. "Now, I've held up my end of the bargain. Please, I beg of you."

She leaned to him, put her arm around his shoulder, and squeezed him as hard as she could.

Releasing him, she sat at his desk, typed in a couple of commands on her MacBook Air, connected it to his printer, and watched as dozens of pages flowed to his desk.

"I wish you continued success in the military, Roy," she said as she began to walk away. She took two steps and turned to Perkins. "You know all those pages by themselves will not help you."

He looked at her in surprise.

"Those pages came from two computers, one belonging to Lt. Moss, and the other from an ISIS mole. Have their homes searched and their computers confiscated."

"Right on, but the jihadists are smart, they'll—"

"I don't consider anyone very bright who clings to the lifestyle of the fifth century, as all these people do, but they will indeed try to protect their secrets and they don't mind killing themselves to protect those secrets. Make sure that both Moss and her cohort are apprehended at the same moment as their homes are searched. I'll bet there are other jihadists in both their residences who'll blow up those computers on a one-second notice." She pointed at the pages on Perkin's desk. "Those papers are probably of no help to you in a court of law. The only things that'll save your ass are the intact computers with that information in them."

Chapter 22

Farok's Hangar
Aden, Yemen
4:00 p.m.

FAROK'S 747 WITH THE Kazakhstan Air logo was moved to a corner to make room for his recently manufactured, high-altitude balloon, which stretched for over 100 feet across the floor. The ten-man crew had just folded the silver polyethylene film into a bundle, three feet in diameter. Fully inflated in the stratosphere, the balloon would be 100 feet wide, 100 feet tall, and filled with almost 10,000 cubic feet of helium.

Sven Mobris walked over to Farok just as the small, clean-shaven man entered the hangar, wearing a white tuxedo, sans tie, and smelling of Frederic Malle cologne.

Sven rubbed his hands together as he talked, eager to describe all the modifications he'd made on the balloon.

Farok looked at his nails and rubbed a spot from one, shifted his weight several times, and rubbed his hands over his smooth, moist facial skin.

The fast-talking balloon expert went on and on, describing his work. As the soliloquy came to an end, Farok finally interrupted him. "Yes, yes, yes—is the flight on schedule?"

"My manager has made all the arrangements. Is that agreeable?"

"Perfect," Farok said.

Sven began to rub his hands together again. "The only question I have about the flight is the nature of the 'scientific instruments.' They are a little heavy, at 960 pounds, and combined with the 236 pounds of the aviator, we're pushing a nearly 1,200-pound payload."

"Is that a problem?"

"The polyethylene film is plenty strong enough, and the capsule and rigging are good, but I'll have to place an extra tank of helium aboard. The extra weight will slow the lift time."

"How much?"

"It'll take about twenty minutes to make 10,000 feet, maybe a little less. After that, throwing the empty helium canister over will allow the rest of the flight to go on schedule, to 100,000 feet."

"It won't over inflate and burst?"

"No. I promise that. It'll go only one way, up."

Farok's face turned red as he stood on his toes to put his face in Sven's face. "That balloon pops—and you're history."

Sven stepped away and shivered at the chilling implications of the threat. He started to speak, then turned and went back to his work.

Farok smiled as he witnessed the fear he'd instilled into the man.

Farok's Offices
Aden, Yemen
4:55 p.m.

JACK FISHER WAS JUST bundling his papers to leave when Farok strolled in from his foray to the hangar.

"Perhaps you'd like to read an obituary," Farok said, handing Fisher a photocopy of the posting, with a picture of Fisher at the top.

"What's this?" he asked, after seeing his photograph.

"Just read."

"World renowned nuclear physicist, Jack Fisher, was killed today when his plane crashed in the Swiss Alps." He looked up. "Is this some sort of joke?"

"Just continue."

Fisher read of the degrees he'd earned, the research awards he'd won, the universities where he'd taught, the awards he'd won in nuclear physics, and on and on. He looked up and shook his head. "Tell me what this is all about."

"Read the last paragraph."

Fisher read aloud, "His wife, Sarah Cummings, two teen age daughters, Daphne and Marsha, and his twenty-year-old son, Frederick, died in the private plane crash with him."

Fisher paled as he looked into the barrel of Farok's pistol.

"Most people don't have the opportunity I've afforded you—to see their own death notice."

Fisher clasped his hands in front of him. "Please don't shoot me. I have so much to offer the world."

Farok gestured with his pistol. "On your knees."

But Fisher continued to stand and beg for his life.

Farok's hands were shaking so badly, he held the gun in both hands. *BOOM!*

Fisher fell to his knees and looked down at the blood pouring from his chest. "Get a doctor! I don't want to die!"

"You die as poorly as the peasants I've executed," Farok said, casually. "I thought with an intellectual, it would be different."

Farok raised the gun to Fisher's face and pulled the trigger. The engineer and physicist slumped over and sprawled out on the floor of the office.

Farok, now proud of himself, sat at his desk and rubbed both hands together until they were still, then outstretched both hands before him. "I'm as steady as a rock."

Chapter 23

Day 11
Jackson City Hospital
Jackson City, North Carolina
10:16 a.m.

JACQUES JACOBO, "JAKJAK" TO his friends, finished his coffee and began transporting his last patient of the day from the X-ray department to her room. As he pushed the young woman on the gurney, she asked him, "How long does it take to finish your Radiology Technician course and go back to Haiti?"

He took a deep breath. "It ees only one years."

"You know, in wheeling a stretcher like this, and talking with patients, like you have to do, it would be better if you spoke proper English. There are English classes in the city that you could take and soon be proficient. Why don't you think about it?"

Jakjak frowned and silently delivered his patient before finishing his shift.

Jakjak was tired of being treated like he was stupid. He made the long walk to his dorm room and upon entering, kicked the bed. "Damn beech," he said. "I graduated from de best college in Haiti, and she say I doan no how to talk."

He was so happy to be finished for the day. Even lying around in his room was better than the X-ray school. He'd led an exciting life prior to this, working as the bodyguard for Haiti's Minister of Finance. He'd done that interesting job for fifteen years and it had challenged him every day. With the many problems that the Minister had faced in controlling the Finances of Haiti, he'd constantly sought Jakjak's advice.

Jakjak had come to the United States at the invitation of his friend, Dr. Scott James. He was living now in North Carolina. Scott James had invited him there to learn how to be an X-ray tech, but he was bored and disinterested in X-rays, and even more so, angered on a daily basis by people treating him like he was a child. He wasn't a child. He was very smart, and people like Dr. James respected him, a fact that brought him a small sense of satisfaction.

Jakjak was tall and muscular, so much so that he looked like he could start for the local sports team right away, even though he was pushing forty years of age. His English was indeed flawed, but he was trying, and quite frankly he felt that in just a few months he'd learned to speak better than many of the foreign aid workers in Haiti had learned to speak French even after years in his country.

With Dr. James in protective custody in Quantico, Jakjak was more or less on his own. The police, FBI, and CIA who seemed to accompany Scott James everywhere, were suddenly gone.

Scott James' unfortunate entanglement with ISIS terrorists had spilled over into Jakjak's life, a thing he both like and hated. On the one hand, it was exciting. He liked Scott James and Elizabeth Keyes. On the other hand, the three of them together, along with a lot of other people, had become involved in a very deadly game.

Which could make a person paranoid.

There was no denying that for two nights in a row, Jakjak had seen a black-suited man sitting on a park bench near the hospital dorm, reading a newspaper for what seemed like hours. This man didn't look like one of Farok's men. He was white and had spiked blond hair. That didn't necessarily mean anything. Jakjak's years as a bodyguard had taught him to expect the unexpected. Anybody could be a terrorist these days, and Farok was well-known to have operatives of all stripes.

Fed up with his life and situation, Jakjak was ready to go on the offensive. He decided that he was going to go for a walk, and if he saw the stranger out there he would either call the police or confront the man, or both. In the tangled world of Scott James and Elizabeth Keyes, a world he was very much a part of, assumed innocence wasn't a luxury he could afford.

He left the dorm room, walked down the hall, and then went out the door. He walked across the grounds of the hospital and sure enough spotted the stranger sitting on the bench, pretending to read the paper.

Jakjak could take any man alive. He was that tough. He also had his pistol underneath his jacket. That helped. The question now was: Is this guy part of American Law Enforcement, or is he an ISIS operative? Jakjak slipped his hand into his jacket and unsnapped the strap of his shoulder holster.

His walked to the bench and stood, glaring at the blond-headed man in the black suit.

"Ah," the stranger said, smiling, "Jakjak. So nice to see you. You look fit, as usual."

Stunned, Jakjak shot back, "Who are you?"

"A friend."

Jakjak looked around quickly, scanning three hundred and sixty degrees for threats.

"Monsieur Jacobo, we are, well, somewhat concerned about the predicament of your colleague, Dr. James." The stranger put down his paper and pulled out a cigarette. He lit up, and blew smoke at Jakjak. "There are ... There are, how should we say: Too many corruptions."

"What ees dis? Are you smoking marijuana? Who are you?"

The stranger smiled. "Please don't shout. I have a little news for you."

Instinctively, Jakjak drew his weapon. "You die here," he said.

"No, I don't think so," the freakish man said, smiling. "Jakjak, my friend, we've been watching you for over two weeks now. Your life is in grave danger. We know a terrorist cell is somewhere nearby, preparing to attack. We were hoping to wait and draw them out, but things have been complicated by the fact that I am needed elsewhere."

The tall Haitian didn't budge.

"Well, a little suspicion on your part is quite understandable," the stranger said, amiably, and then took another long drag on the joint. "I must go now, but I do need to warn you: Various unsavory elements are tracking you, and you are in serious danger if you stay here."

"What 'unsavory elements'? Who de fock do yu work for? You are Farok's people! I keel yu now!"

The man was completely unperturbed. "Oh, no. I am with you and the good doctor. My people have an interest in getting to Farok. We'd like him eliminated. The only time he comes up for air is when he's trying to kill Scott James—and of course possess beautiful Elizabeth. That is quite helpful to our organization."

"CIA."

The man laughed. "No." He got up slowly, brushed off his pants, and said, "Jakjak, my friend, watch your back. If I know where you are and where you go, then Farok does, too. You must leave this place." He waved goodbye and walked down the sidewalk.

Jakjak stood there, stunned. Being Scott James' friend was exciting, yes, but this was just plain weird. He quickly took out his own cell phone and dialed Elizabeth Keyes.

"Come to Quantico," she said, without hesitation. Clearly, the man was the same freak-of-a-guy who had confronted Scott in jail. "And Jakjak," she added, "don't go to Scott's house or use Scott's car. Go to my safe-deposit box and get some money and buy a car, I mean a real car. Get some serious wheels and get here as fast as you can."

Chapter 24

Cadet Dorm
FBI Training Center
Quantico
11:22 a.m.

"THIS DOESN'T NECESSARILY MEAN that there's some tampering going on here," Josh said, as he looked at the death photo. "I'm not sure what it proves. One thing is for sure, we have to get a real pro to look at this picture."

"Perkins said that it's authentic," Keyes said.

"That's not going to help up in a court of law. In fact, I doubt if we can even *use* this in a court of law."

"A second gun was fired!" I blurted out.

Keyes nodded. "Perkins said that the second gun was

a .45, but it was held against the chest. The man's chest absorbed all the contact and there was no impact with any air mass, so the sound would probably be quieter."

"Be careful of your sources of evidence," Josh said, sternly. "Illegally acquired material will be disallowed in a Federal Court, and could even result in Keyes being prosecuted."

As he said this, I stiffened.

"It would help if you found this 'Emmanuel' character," Josh said. "If you produced this Emmanuel guy—if you found him—you could basically turn the whole case upside down."

I nodded, then went to the kitchen to check on Scotty. He was busy with a newspaper puzzle.

"Whatcha' doing?" I asked.

My question failed to interrupt his concentration.

Elizabeth answered for him. "The Celebrity Ciphers."

I looked over his shoulder to see half the words penciled in. "That's the encryption game. It's too tough for a ten year-old."

Elizabeth put her finger over her lips. "Shh."

I shrugged. I saw this game in the paper every time I turned to the comic section. I could do crosswords and the Sudoku, but never got to first base with Celebrity Ciphers.

I turned to go out but Scotty spoke up. "Elizabeth taught me how to do this. Look, Dad, I've finished half of it and it's starting to go fast now."

I leaned and looked. He'd written a lot of figures on the paper beside the puzzle.

"It's really easy. You see, the E, T, and A's are the most common letters in the English language, the 'E' is 12 % of

The Encryption Game

all letters written, the 'T', 9 %, and the 'A', 8 %. The 'O' comes in fourth."

"So, how does that help you?"

"I always find the single-letter words, and they are either 'I' or 'A'. And, lots of A's and I's have apostrophes after them, like here, O'XX. The O has to be I and the double X is LL."

I smiled at his enthusiasm. "But what about all the other letters in the alphabet?"

"Well, this one was easy because I figured out the A and the L, in the word All. The name of the author of the quote in the cipher has the letters AL—AL—A."

"Who's that?"

"I didn't know, so I went to the Internet, typed in those letters, and the Internet filled in the blanks. Alan Alda. I don't know who he is, but he's a real person, and from that, I know the A's, L's, N's, and D's. Then, I take the three-letter words and try to piece them together and soon..."

I looked at Elizabeth and smiled. "So, you'll make him into a decryption expert, just like you."

Elizabeth was great with my kids. "It's called frequency theory. It's the basis for most decryption methods. Certain letters and words appear in messages far more frequently than others. That is one thing that is impossible to hide."

Chapter 25

Jackson City Hospital
Jackson City, North Carolina
6:46 p.m.

JAKJAK ENTERED HIS ROOM, turned on every light, and packed his small suitcase. He stuffed all his worldly belongings in the case, including the two hundred thousand dollars he'd gotten from the safe-deposit box, and his Glock, 9mm automatic.

Jakjak knew where his stalkers would probably be: parked in the lot near his apartment. If he could just slip out without anyone noticing, he might be able to sneak up on whoever was following him. He tiptoed to the back hallway, on the opposite side of the dorm from the employee parking lot. He slipped out the second story window, slid down the gutter, and hugged the dark building until he reached a dumpster, which was ideal cover.

Jakjak peeked around the dumpster. They were there, that much was obvious. There were two men in a dark SUV. They were black men, built like body builders, probably Congolese.

But Jacques Jacobo was cocky. He was pro. He knew he could whip them in a fight. The hospital shift change had occurred an hour before, so there would be little traffic in the area for a couple of hours.

Jakjak stayed flat against the building, creeping along the side. One of the Congolese slipped from the car and walked quietly to the back dorm door, only a few yards from where Jakjak stood.

Jakjak watched as the man pulled a crowbar from his tool bag and slipped it in the chain that locked the door to the dorm. The hulking Congolese man raised his hand to smack the flat end of the bar, trying to force the door open. For a moment, he stopped, as if we were anticipating someone exiting the building. When nothing happened, he pushed the door open enough to stick his head in.

Jakjak threw a coke bottle at the SUV. As it sailed through the air, he lurched to the door, grabbed the handle, and slammed the door against the man's neck. He heard a quick, brittle, *snap*, at the same moment that the bottle hit the SUV.

Jakjak shoved the man inside the door, took his pistol and the crowbar, slipped on the guy's black sport coat, bowed his head, and walked leisurely back to the SUV.

There, Jakjak got in the passenger side front seat and put his Glock in the driver's face. The surprised man threw his hands up.

"Who awh you and why awh you hee-ah!" Jakjak shouted.

"Fuck you," was the response.

Jakjak slammed the sharp end of the crowbar in the man's ribs. "Leesten, fock face! If you weesh to be alive, talk."

The Congolese man looked at his bloodied side and started to lower his hand.

Jakjak dropped the gun to the man's thigh and pulled the trigger.

The man screamed in pain.

"One more chance: Why aw yu try-ink to keel me?"

"The Grand Emir told us to kill you."

"Wrong answer," Jakjak said. He raised his Glock to the man's face and pulled the trigger.

With his attackers dead, Jakjak, the professional, stripped the bodies and vehicle of any intel he could find. There were three cell phones among the dead.

Exotic Cars of Jackson City
Jackson City, North Carolina
7:00 p.m.

AT 7:00 P.M., JAKJAK walked into Exotic Cars of Jackson City, right as they were closing. The adrenaline was still pumping in his veins. He knew he had to act fast. There was no way that Farok would send only one team to do his business. Jakjak needed to get a car, some real wheels, and get the cell phones to Quantico, fast.

Beautiful cars of all types filled the showroom floor, Porches, Lamborghinis, Bentleys, Aston Martins. It seemed like they'd packed every used car they could possibly find into one dealership. There must have been ten million dollars' worth of shiny machines parked inside.

A salesman, a short fellow with a goatee and a big belly, stood up from his desk at the far end of the open-air facility, and walked over briskly. "Dave Smith. And what is your name, Sir?"

"My name is Jacques Jacobo."

"How are you, Mr. Jacobo. Is there something we can help you with?"

"I need to purchase an automobile."

"Well, you've come to the right place," Smith laughed, "We carry the finest cars in the world."

"I see. De are all berry nice. But I have special needs, you see. Do you have any that have been modified for gubamint officials?"

"Eh... Modified... For... Government...?"

"Yes. Do you have any-tink with armor plating?"

"Uh..."

"I have a longk back-groun in gub-a-mint security, and I am he-ah to get some-tink for a client who needs added protection."

Smith looked up at the impressive, muscular, Jakjak, and wondered what trouble this man was brewing. "Well..."

"Because of the urgent natcha ub my bidniss, Mr. Smith, I weesh to pay cash."

"Well. Uh... Do you want a limousine? Or—"

The Encryption Game

"No. I need some-tink with speed."

"Well, we have plenty of that here."

"I need metal or composite side armor and bullet proof or bullet resistant glass. I also need room for three people."

A shout came from the other side of the room. "Show him the Evora!"

The man who had just yelled strode over to Jakjak and said, "Ed Finley. I'm the owner. I have the car you're looking for, but it's in the back. It does have some armor in the side body and the kind of glass you're looking for. It's an older model. We don't keep it out here because we just don't get a lot of requests for this type of automobile and it takes up space."

"What is it?"

"It's a Lotus Evora. It's a 2010 model. I believe it's got about 12,000 miles on it. But it's a rocket ship. It's like a missile. Three hundred and forty-five horses under the hood and almost zero body weight. It will take a corner unlike anything you've ever seen. It's probably the best handling car here."

"I take it."

"Uh... Terrific. It'll take a few minutes to get it ready." The owner shook Jakjak's hand and turned to his salesman. "Dave, why don't you get this gentleman started with his paperwork? You said that this is going to be cash?"

Jakjak patted his shoulder bag, filled with Elizabeth Keyes' assassination money, and said, "Yes. Cash."

At Smith's desk, Jakjak went through the laborious process of signing the mountain of paperwork. "You realize, of course," the salesman said, "that cash transactions of over a few thousand dollars are monitored by the federal government."

"I understand. There is no problem there."

The salesman glanced up at the television in the lounge area, then looked at Jakjak and said, shaking his head, "What happens to people, right?"

Jakjak glanced at the silent television. CNN was showing the same news loop they'd been playing every twenty minutes since the day of the shooting. It was a shot of Dr. Scott James' hospital ID photo, with the caption, "Crazed shooter was plastic surgeon. Life went downhill."

"This guy, this Scott James guy: He was always kind of a nut. But in a good way. But I guess—"

"Yu know Dokte James?"

"I know *of* him. Everybody around here does. True story: One year, this guy, this Dr. James guy, he takes a brand new Winnebago and transforms it into his own private hospital. Like an operating room on wheels. And he goes off into the boonies, way up in the mountains, and he just starts doing operations on poor folks. I mean, like people back in the sticks who've never been to a doctor in their whole lives. People with facial deformities. Like fixing hair-lips and stuff. All kinds of stuff. He just did it cuz he felt like doin' it. Supposedly he was really good at it. Kind of an artist with a scalpel. Made the papers. There are people out in the boonies who actually named their kids after him. 'Scott James Jones'—shit like that. Now look at him. Crazy idiot. What happens to people? Once a nut, always a nut, I guess. I bet some of those people'll want to change their names, now. Sheeesh! What a moron."

A roar exploded from the back of the dealership, an aggressive, tightly-wound engine noise that shattered the peaceful afternoon, *WHOOM! WHOOM!*

"Okay, Mr. Jacobo, sounds like they've got that Lotus ready for ya.'"

Chapter 26

Elkins Regional Airport
Elkins, West Virginia
Midnight

THEY ARRIVED IN A thunderstorm, a convoy of mud-plastered motor vehicles, rumbling down Highway 250, bound for Airport Lane. At Elkins Regional, they continued to the fourth hangar from the street, Hangar D.

Larry Waltrip had been waiting for them. He stood now at his office window and watched the unusual array of trucks pass. The first was a rusted Ford 150. That was followed by a triple-axle logging truck, modified with a fourth axle, hauling a fifty-foot-long trailer with an irregularly shaped cargo loaded on it, wrapped in half-a-dozen tattered tarps, lashed together with hemp rope.

The humps and bumps of the road seemed to make the whole thing come alive. The load flexed and rolled with the truck's movement, and the loose edges of the canvas flapped in the breeze so that the whole thing looked like an immense spine. Sitting on the logging trailer was a hoist, a huge crane with steel jaws, so that the whole irregular shape gave off the eerie feeling of being like a Chinese dragon.

The third vehicle looked like an antique model of a Brinks truck, armored, with small windows and heavy tires. Waltrip tried to catch the eyes of the drivers, but they looked solemnly ahead and kept driving. The whole procession was too much for the airport owner. He stepped out of his office and tried to hale someone, anyone, to stop.

At last, a cammo-painted, 1957 Chevy pickup stopped beside Waltrip and the single occupant opened the passenger side door. "Hop in," the driver said.

Waltrip got in and reached to shake the man's hand. The guy's hands never left the steering wheel. Waltrip withdrew his hand and looked at the man's eyes, still in an uninterested focus on the vehicles driving ahead.

Waltrip said in his deep voice, "Shit, man. Nasty day to be driving. Where did you come from, Front Royal?"

"Nope."

Waltrip frowned and looked at the small man beside him, wearing a grease smeared T-shirt featuring a skull and crossbones, and black cotton pants held up by a string belt. Other than a four inch, jagged scar on his forehead, the man's face was quite smooth, white from a lack of exposure to the sun, and totally void of emotion. Waltrip crossed his arms and looked out the side window, determined to wait for this dickhead to respond, and if not, to call the local police.

He reached for the door handle to leave when the driver finally opened his mouth. "I'm Mack. I suppose you want your money?"

Waltrip cleared his throat and spoke loudly. "If you plan to stay for more than five minutes, I expect to see your money." Frowning, he leaned toward Mack. "And it better be in a form I can verify with your bank."

Mack pointed to the glove compartment. "It's in there."

Waltrip looked back and forth between the man's stone cold face and the glove compartment before opening it. He sat back in surprise as he saw bundles of cash.

"It's all there," Mack said.

Waltrip counted one of the thousand-dollar packets of hundred dollar bills, then casually inspected the other nine packets.

Waltrip lowered his head as he asked in a low voice, "You always this easy to get along with?"

Mack's expression never changed. "It's been a long week. Just give me the key to our hangar."

"What if I just ride down with you and show you around?"

"Not necessary. Everybody's had a rough couple of days." Anger flashed briefly on Mack's face. "And just like me, they want to be left alone." A calmness returned to his face as he held out his hand without looking away from the road. "I'll take the key."

Waltrip was mad, mad enough to withdraw his contract and boot them from his premises. But he was a little afraid of these guys. There was something sinister about this group. He looked at the fist full of money, which he badly needed to make payroll for the week, and finally passed on the key.

Waltrip got out at the next stop. He ran through the rain and entered his office, put on a slicker, and drove his ten-year-old Land Rover to Hangar D. He parked by the side entrance and quietly opened the door with his key, just to look in. He looked into the face of a white man with a shaved head and a lot bigger and stronger than Mack. He held a .45 in his hand, dropped to his side.

"Could I see your boss?" Waltrip asked.

"He couldn't make it," the big fellow said, and then closed the door in Waltrip's face.

Waltrip stood in the rain, trying to come to grips with what he'd seen going on behind the door guard: All four of the vehicles were parked inside. The logging hoist on the truck, the jaws of the dragon, was straining to lift a forty foot-long bundle, while one guy, the apparent leader, was dressed in a starched, pleated, short-sleeved dress shirt with a revolver in a side holster.

Waltrip shivered. Before today, all his usual balloon crews and mechanics had been bright, smiley faced young men and women, as eager to talk as they were to listen to Waltrip's advice. These people left him cold.

Chapter 27

Day 12
Cadet Dorm
FBI Training Center
Quantico
11:01 a.m.

MY PHONE RANG. IT was Jakjak's cell. "Jakjak, I've missed you. How's your job going?"

He bypassed the question and said, "I was attacked. Farok's men."

"Are you in Quantico?"

I could hear him laugh as he said, "Yes, I queet my job and come to help you. I arrife hee-ah lass nite."

That stunned me. I got him his green card and placed

him in a secure job at Jackson City Hospital.

I took a deep breath and responded. "I don't think the Marine base here will let you come in. I'm going to send Elizabeth to talk to you. It may take awhile, an hour or so."

Starbucks Coffee
Quantico, Virginia
12:04 p.m.

KEYES GREETED JAKJAK WITH a warm hug. She squeezed him tightly and almost didn't let go. It was so good to see a friendly face.

Jakjak told her of his encounter with Farok's operatives.

After a movement, she asked, "Where are your 'friends' now?"

"Dey likes pretty rocks. Dey awr looking up at a pretty one down de road a piece."

She laughed. "Will they be rock-watching very long?"

He smiled and shook his head. "Dey awr so far from de street, nobody gonna take dem from dat rock in this century."

Elizabeth knew Haitian patois, and she knew that Jakjak was saying he'd buried his attackers. Even more, she knew that Jakjak was a pro. She asked, quickly, "Their cell phones. Did they have cell phones?"

"Oui, Mademoiselle. Dey had three phones between dem. I brought dem all to you." He took the phones from his pocket and handed them to her. "Dose two Samsungs came from the bigger man of the two."

She jumped from her chair and hugged Jakjak.

The Encryption Game

He laughed, "I know how much you like de phones of terrorists!"

Keyes leaned over one of the phones and worked away for nearly ten minutes before looking up. "They're locked. I need the passwords. I need the pass codes. That'll take a while, even with the apps I have." She looked intently at Jakjak. "Did you remove anything else from the bodies? Anything on which they might have written a pass code?"

He smiled. "I emptied de coats, de pockets, and searched de entire car. Dis is what I found."

There were dozens of scraps of paper, two wallets, a car title, and insurance papers. She opened the first wallet and scanned the driver's license.

Jakjak pointed at the photo in the first wallet. "Dat ees de worker, not de leader."

Elizabeth looked up. "It's a North Carolina license but it's been forged, I can tell."

"How do you know that? It looks fine to me."

She laughed. "One of my jobs in the past was creating fake ID papers, a lot of them for my own use. This one's OK, but not of great quality. I could have spotted it across the room."

She took out twenty-six American dollars and handed it to Jakjak. "He won't need this under his rock. Use it to buy lunch."

Jakjak chuckled a little. Typical Elizabeth.

She looked at the second wallet, from the leader of the two men. This one had a fist full of hundred dollar bills and a wad of lesser bills. She smiled a little and gave the money to Jakjak. "This is Farok's money, blow it."

He smiled and placed the thick wad of currency in

his wallet. "Someday we put Farok unda de rock, oui Mademoiselle?"

"Oui, my friend."

She continued to scrutinize the bits of paper and documents. "Nothing apparent," she said.

Jakjak was on the edge of his seat as he watched everything Elizabeth did, looking at every item and each scrap of paper with her critical eye.

Finally, she took the empty wallets and turned them inside out. Nothing. "Okay. Why don't you get a motel and stay nearby. We'll be in touch. We're actually trying to get out of the FBI dorm and get some air, but I don't know if they're going to let us."

"Oui, Mademoiselle." Jakjak pointed to the bad-assed, low-slung, black Lotus Evora, parked at the curb. "What do you tink of our new wheels?"

Keyes smiled wickedly. "I like'em a lot."

Cadet Dorm
FBI Training Center
Quantico
2:02 p.m.

"I HAVE TO GET the passwords to these phones," she said.

"What if they're ten digits? With a special character?"

"Then it will take forever. I'll have to get in touch with my friends. But there is one thing that could help us right now: When you have complex passwords, you usually have them written down. People just can't remember them. But I'm not seeing anything. We have to go over every scrap of paper here and try to find something."

"Maybe it's his driver's license number. Or maybe it's his car title number or something."

"Even if we exhausted all of the obvious possibilities, but he has just one special character, or if he's changed one component to lower case or upper case, then even with my apps, we've got nothing. Sweaty bastards."

"What?"

"This wallet stinks. This guy must have carried it in his gym shorts."

I picked up the wallet and smelled it. "Smells like cowhide to me." I picked up the other bits of paper, one by one, and sniffed. "Sweat. Sweat. Tobacco smoke. Serious sweat. This matchbook here smells like urine, though."

"What?"

"That's not sweat, it's urine."

"What? You're saying he pissed on his matches?"

"I don't what he did, but I'm a doctor. I know a little about the human body, including the fluids it secretes, and this guy got some urine on his matches."

I saw her gasp. She grabbed the matchbook out of my hand and held it up in the light.

"I didn't say you could *see it*. Unless the body is dehydrated, urine is usually clear."

"Clear," she said, quietly.

Keyes ripped out a match and frantically lit it. Once it had caught, she held the matchbook cover over the flame and slowly moved the paper in a circular fashion to keep it from catching fire. As the paper heated, a series of brown numbers started to materialize before our eyes.

"Yeah!" Keyes shouted. "Urine!"

More and more, what had once been a blank white

space, was becoming, crisp, clear, brown numbers. "Yeah!" Keyes screamed.

"Holy shit," I said. "Somebody just made a mistake."

"Oldest trick in the book! Invisible ink! Spy craft 101! This guy couldn't remember his pass code so he dipped a toothpick or something in his urine and wrote it out on this! We got it!"

She held up the open matchbook so that I could see it better, and started reading, "X-O-5-0-Z-%. See the lines drawn over the X and Z? That probably means lower case."

"But are you sure that's his password? That could be *anything*."

"We're about to find out."

Keyes grabbed one of the cell phones and carefully punched in the code. Nothing. "Shit." She grabbed the second and punched in the code. The screen transformed to an animation for AT&T. "Brilliant!"

Cadet Dorm
FBI Training Center
Quantico
Midnight

KEYES SAT AT THE table, working through the phones and writing on a yellow legal pad, while Scotty sat on the other side, working out Celebrity Ciphers.

My sons adored Elizabeth. They had no idea what she was. I'm not sure it would've mattered, because she was quickly becoming their mother. She was very good with them, a real natural. But there was something terrible about it. I loved them so much, and I loved Elizabeth, too.

But seeing them grow up as essentially prisoners of the law enforcement, targets, pawns, broke my heart.

After a while, Scotty took his paper and held it up, to show Elizabeth.

She feigned surprise. "Have you finished that already?"

He bowed his head and looked at the table. "I... I think. Is there a real person named Jimmy," he spelled out the last name, "F A L L O N?"

"Why, yes. Jimmy Fallon's a guy who has a TV show on every night."

Scotty looked up at her and smiled. "Then, I got it right! I did it like you said! There were two sets of double letters, two ciphers that were repeated, like you showed me!"

She beamed at him. "Not bad. Not bad at all."

"Frequency theory," I said.

"Good, Scott. You're learning. Repetition is the Achilles Heel of cryptographers. Anything that repeats, especially things like double letters, is a weakness in the cipher. Even the German's enigma machine couldn't hide things like doubles letters or repeated words forever. It's the easiest way to decipher, essentially."

"And you, young lady?" I said, standing over her, acting like a schoolteacher. "How is *your* decryption going? Hmm?"

"You're a real comedian, Scott," she said, dropping her pencil to the table. "I'm beat. I'll have to do some of this tomorrow."

I sat at the table and looked at the scribbles on her legal pad. "What've you got so far?"

There was a lengthy series of letters, each with a

number written over them. "What is all this stuff? It's impenetrable gibberish."

"It's cipher text. It's mono-alphabetic Caesar shift. It's the last layer of Farok's encryption."

Scotty stared at her, rapt in amazement—and understanding. I, on the other hand, was completely confused. "Could you give that to me again, in English?"

"Each letter of the alphabet is assigned a corresponding letter, like here," she pointed to a G on the page. "That's actually an 'A'. But the next time they want to use the letter A, they've written the letter M. There's a shift. The first time they wanted to express A, they counted six places down the alphabet and wrote 'G'. The second time they wanted to express A, they counted thirteen places, and wrote 'M'. They shift the number of places down the alphabet each time they repeat a letter. The trick is to figure out the number of places down the line they're shifting. It's a simple type of cipher, but it does take time to crack, and time is always the problem with code breaking. The beauty of it is that if you're the organization who is using it, your people only have to memorize one mathematical formula—the shift."

"This guy couldn't remember his password."

"That's because he was probably changing his password every day. The formula for the shift is a one time deal."

"So what does it say?"

Elizabeth's drooping eyes and slouched posture betrayed her all night vigil. I started making her some coffee.

"It basically says that they're talking about an EMP.

The Encryption Game

Have you ever heard of Electro Magnetic Pulse?"

I nodded. "Yes, it's the EMP that the papers have mentioned several times that scares everybody to death."

"Correct. A nuclear bomb creates a lot of gamma radiation which ionizes atoms in the atmosphere, creating free electrons that fill the atmosphere. The electrons are deflected by the magnetic field of the planet and make a huge electromagnetic pulse, the E1. The E1 creates high voltages, like 50,000 volts per meter, in anything electrical, and melts most of the electrical wires. It's like a giant sunspot.

"Let me read you the stuff I'm sure about so far: 'When the explosion happens, everything with an electrical connection will be stopped.' Or, at least that's what I think it says. But it does say E-M-P in several places. So I feel certain about the electrical stuff."

"The bomb in Nagasaki did that. But I think you have to have a high-altitude detonation to pose a real EMP risk without destroying everything on the ground, right?"

"Yes. High-altitude is usually the way the scenario is portrayed."

"Then we need help in finding Farok's rocket delivery system before it's too late. I should call General Perkins."

"Maybe. But there's no message that says this is the actual plan, and there's no date given for when all this is supposed to occur. We should try to get a little more info before we cry wolf again."

Keyes went to work relaying to her friends the ISIS messages on the dead man's phone, with the queries, "Is there current information on ISIS plans for an attack in America? Do they have any timetable? Is their focus point

Washington, DC? Will they detonate a nuclear warhead to create an EMP?"

"But," I asked, "there's a whole lot of stuff on this page. Surely that's not all you've deciphered."

"There are a lot of repeats. I've circled them in red. The ciphers are slightly different, but I know what they say, 'missile', 'emp', 'praise God', blah, blah, blah. After a while, you can tell by the order of certain words in the message what the words are most likely to be. They're repeats, what the British in World War II called 'cribs.' You don't have to decipher everything. It takes too long. Again, time is the biggest factor. When the British cracked the Enigma codes in World War II, they frequently only had to crack about half of the message to get its meaning. So, anyway, these seven-lettered words, and these three-lettered words are all the same, they're just repeats, 'missile', and 'emp'."

Scotty was mesmerized by how smart Elizabeth was, but also proud of himself for understanding her.

"Scotty," Keyes said. "Could you give me a moment to talk to your Dad about something private?"

"Okay," he said. He walked over and hugged her and then wandered off down the hall toward his sleeping quarters.

Keyes watched the little guy walk away, then she held up the phone. "I only have the password to this one phone. I have six messages, all going to this man. He was very, very high up in the chain of command. He wasn't just a soldier. Farok or whoever was sending him details."

"Let's hear it."

"The guy with the cell phone is named Nagib. There

are six coded messages from one person, who uses the name Rasur. Apparently, Nagib is new in America in the past two weeks, when the messages start. Rasur directs Nagib to kill Jakjak by shooting him in the abdomen and torturing him into giving the names and address of Dr. James' boys and their attendant. He's also instructed to cut off Jakjak's head."

My knees weakened under me. "I believe Jakjak would die before he said anything."

Elizabeth shook her head. "They are so cruel, they always get their answers." She smiled, "But they won't hurt anybody under the stone."

I had to laugh at that before asking, "Anything else?"

"I'm surprised. That was his only directive, to get information from Jakjak, then kill him. The last message tells them to drive to Chicago after Jakjak is killed."

"Strange, to bring him to this area, just to do that one thing. Where is the guy, Rasur, who sent the orders?"

"I can't pinpoint his location, but he's apparently directing three other guys. I don't have the other pass codes, but I've plugged them in my Apps and I'm trying to learn them."

I leaned over her shoulder and read: "'Saint Francis sends a Christian blessing.' These soldiers were all Muslims. Why was a Christian message sent to those guys?"

"It's a code."

"'Four score and seven years ago.'"

"Gettysburg Address. More code. That one is repeated in several places."

"That's all? Isn't there more?"

"Yes. There's more. But I'm exhausted."

I thought for a moment. "I'm not catholic, but I believe St. Francis of Assisi was the Saint of birds and animals. I see statues of him in gardens, holding a rabbit, with a bird on his shoulder. Birds make me think of Twitter, but animals and rabbits? I can't come up with anything."

"The bird. Twitter. I thought of that and looked on Twitter. That was popular with ISIS for a while, but not so now. They're almost exclusively on WhatsApp now. The rabbits and animals, I'm drawing a blank on that one. I'm not sure all of this stuff has meaning. Some of it could be a hoax. The Gettysburg Address, the blessing of the Saint—tough to say."

Chapter 28

Day 13
Suburban Apartment
Philadelphia, Pennsylvania
8:00 a.m.

THREE BEARDED MEN IN their early twenties, two from Pakistan and one from a small town in Montana, knocked lightly on the apartment door. Amahn Alahahd ran through a tiny living room crowded by an open sleeper sofa and two side chairs. Two teenage boys were sleeping and a woman was nursing a baby, with two children in diapers at her side.

Amahn opened the door slightly, whispered a few words, then escorted the three men to a small bedroom, where an elderly man and woman were sleeping side by side in a single bed.

Amahn clapped his hands. The man and woman, dressed in their underwear, sprang from the bed and left. Amahn locked the door and spoke in a whisper. "How many men have you recruited?"

The group's spokesman replied, "One hundred forty."

"I have four men who came with me from the Syrian Refugee group. They are well trained and have combat experience in Afghanistan and Syria. They will direct the activities of your group. Do you have access to trucks?"

"Yes. There are three parked in my neighborhood and I can start them. I copied their keys."

"Your trucks are needed to carry the local jihadists to the point of attack. I have two school buses to carry the ninety men coming from New York and New Jersey. We'll have to pack them into the buses."

"What's our objective?"

"That is not information you need. Your destination will remain a secret until Wednesday night, when you will gather in Virginia. We must have our people in place before then."

"We come to you as martyrs. Will we die in the attack?"

"Allah will bless you. You will martyr yourselves as you fight to overcome American soldiers."

"But how do we get guns to fight with?"

"That's not your worry. We will have more American M-16's than we need and more bullets than we can fire."

"Will we live?"

"I cannot guarantee that."

Amahn could not divulge any details, a thing the others

understood.

The plan was simple on paper, but plans on paper are not reality. Essentially, the blast would make it possible for a few, brief hours, to overrun a lightly-guarded military facility. The depot in Virginia had twenty-two guards, Farok could hit with over two thousand infantry.

Besides being a spectacular terrorist attack, the biggest ever, by far, the bomb blast would make it impossible for the Americans to coordinate any kind of response for a week or so. And in that week of chaos, everything would change. Within that short time frame, ISIS would seat itself at the big kids' table, permanently.

"Many of you will achieve the martyrdom you wish, and join Allah in Heaven, with all the rewards he has promised his faithful. You will know that the evil men you kill will be rightfully punished, as Allah directs."

The three young men smiled in satisfaction.

Central ISIS Command Post
Gettysburg, Pennsylvania
10:00 a.m.

AS FAST AS THE messages appeared on WhatsApp, Phil Jones photographed them and immediately erased. After a total of twelve were received, he viewed the photos and copied the numbers. He took a pocket calculator and added:

The cells in Pennsylvania: Philadelphia, soldiers, 140; Harrisburg, 210; Quakertown, 163. In South Carolina: North Charleston, 130; Beaufort, 78; Columbia, 112. In Massachusetts: New Bedford, 85; Boston, 97; Harrisburg,

290. In Florida: Palatka 64, Jacksonville, 155.

He transferred the information to the computer, sent it, and immediately erased the message.

Omar Farok's Office
Aden, Yemen
2:10 p.m.

FAROK'S NEW EXECUTIVE ASSISTANT viewed the message, wrote down the numbers, then erased. Farok was lying on his back on the masseuse's table as a shapely, bikini-clad woman rubbed his entire body with a sweet smelling oil. At his head was a second woman, young and gorgeous, and naked, applying cream to his face. Without speaking, Farok's assistant put the card with the numbers in front of his boss' eyes. Farok scanned the card, and said, "We have a great army massing within America. That will ensure the success of our operation."

Naval Barracks
Cape May, Florida
2:30 p.m.

AN ENSIGN WENT TO the officer's toilet and sat on the commode as he typed a WhatsApp message on a Samsung phone he had been issued a month before:

I have 200 weapons and 30,000 rounds of ammunition already on a vehicle ready to deliver to your forces. Give me a time and place for delivery.

He sent the message, then erased it.

The Encryption Game

Omar Farok's Office
Aden, Yemen
3:01 p.m.

Farok's executive assistant received the message from Florida and stored the information before erasing it from his computer. He added it to his inventory and went to Farok, who sat at his desk. Without saying a word, the assistant placed the list on the desk in front of Farok and then stood at attention, waiting for instructions.

Farok ran his tiny, delicate hands over his face, admiring his soft, smooth skin as he reviewed the report. He looked up. "The numbers are adequate except for Washington, DC, and Boston. I expect they'll be joined by the Chicago cell, a force of 300, but with only half the weapons they need. Have our man in Philadelphia take care of that deficit."

"Yes, Grand Emir."

"And, oh, the Chicago cell is bringing a thousand pipe bombs, but I'd feel more comfortable if we supplied them with the US M67 grenades. We have a load of Soviet F1's, but our fighters find the M67s more reliable."

"Yes, Grand Emir. I'll arrange that. Where shall I deliver them?"

"To our warehouses in Newport News."

"None to Norfolk?"

"That's where we'll need them most, but my inventory there is good. With so many military men that have sold weapons to us, we've built a surplus over the past years. But I don't want to move them to other places for fear our big operation in that region will be discovered."

"Should I notify our cells in Mexico and Colorado?"

Farok's face turned red and his left eye began to twitch. He reached into his drawer and pulled out a 9mm pistol, rubbed his hand over it, then laid it on his desk. He looked at the man, expressionless for a moment, then screamed out, "I am the ISIS Commander! I know where every one of my troops is located, and my force, which combined with those I have in place for strikes against the American Devil, as well as my foes in the Middle East, numbers thirty thousand men and women! If I need them, I will order them called! The Mexican jihadists as well as those in Colorado, are loyal to me only as long as I pay them! My other troops work for Allah! They do not complain when they are not given a monthly stipend!"

His assistant ran his finger under his tie and replied, "But all the American jihadists get monetary support from the American government and don't need your money to feed their families. We must give the others wages to maintain their loyalty."

Farok lifted the pistol from the desk and held it flat on his chest. "These people are jihadists and should bow to me as they would to Allah himself."

The assistant began to sweat. "Yes, you are Allah. Your will is my command. I swear never to speak until ordered by you."

Farok pointed the pistol at the quivering man, then abruptly placed it in the drawer. "Tell me when you receive the other messages."

The assistant turned and bounded from the office.

Chapter 29

Day 16
Cadet Dorm
FBI Training Center
Quantico
11:00 a.m.

"We can examine whatever we want while we're here," Josh said as we walked to the laboratory. "But if we want to get an expert involved, we'll have to get copies of the audios from the cell phones. And another thing: We can't tamper or modify or even appear to be tampering or modifying anything."

"Tampering?" I said, "*They're* the ones *tampering*, Josh. Besides, I'm not sure this will help us much," I said. "Like in my experiment, the sound waves will all be of different amplitudes. Also, I'm not exactly sure of what

I'm looking for."

"I've talked to the prosecution about the tampering issue. They've completely clammed up. I'm not sure what's going on. Proving tampering, especially with film or video, can take time."

At the lab, we went through the usual check-in procedure and then we were ushered into a room, where the surly Sergeant Willis brought out a plastic box containing eighteen cell phones and commercial recording decks, the type used by the news media.

The moment Keyes took out the small oscilloscope and headphones, Sergeant Willis' face showed alarm. Suddenly he seemed very uncomfortable. "Uh... before you do that, I'll have to get Mr. Valenti on the phone."

"What do you need to talk to the Prosecutor for?" Josh asked. "We're just listening to the recordings."

"Uh..."

"Stay here. You're the witness."

Willis, now confronted by the sharp Josh Edwards, was uncertain what to do, but it was obvious that he'd been given instructions by someone to watch our every move.

The oscilloscope that Keyes had brought was a smaller model, only slightly bigger than the palm of my hand. The tiny device basically measured pulses—audio pulses, electronic pulses—anything that was too fine to hear or detect with human senses.

I plugged in the little oscilloscope and adjusted the vertical y-axis, which measured the intensity of the sound, and the horizontal x-axis, which measured the time between the pulses, in milliseconds. But it was all so basic. I was clutching at straws, like all desperate people do. They were all staring at me, thinking I was obsessed and half-crazy, I guess. So I ventured a little joke. "If this were an experiment done for a medical text," I said, "the reviewers would discount the study because of the multiple variables. But we're not writing a scientific paper. We're just trying to get my ass out of jail."

Josh and Elizabeth burst out laughing.

"Well," Josh said, "at least you know."

I fine-tuned the signal, which I'd leave constant for all the sounds, and lowered the distraction of the excessive background noise. After I was satisfied with the settings, I began to listen to the eighteen recordings, which were loaded, five at a time, into the little oscilloscope.

Elizabeth was patient as I closed my eyes and listened.

After a moment, I took out a large piece of graph paper that the kids used for their homework and centered an X to designate the spot where Emmanuel fell. Using the information provided with the cell phones, I slowly drew a schematic, illustrating where the sounds came from. I put a label on every one of the points on the graph paper.

With that in place, I began my analysis. "If you notice the captions, there was no uniformity of the phones that received the sounds. There were Samsungs, Apples, Nokias, Sonys, LG's, Blackberrys, and Motorolas in the group."

Elizabeth jumped ahead of me. "The amplitudes, the loudness of these—they're so variable—they don't help us at all."

"C'mon, Elizabeth. You must equate the amplitude of the recordings to the distance from the gun that I shot. The phones farther away showed a diminishing sound volume."

She looked down and said quietly, "I knew that."

I laughed and hugged her. "That was cute. But there's a second sound recorded in some of the readings. And it's constant over the residual background noise."

"Uh," Willis interjected, "That's the echoes. You know—all those buildings in Williamsburg. Uh...That's like an echo or something."

I glanced over at Willis. Even *he* didn't believe that.

"No," I said. "A second shot was fired. That's a different round. That's like a .45 or something, but muffled."

I returned to the oscilloscope and listened for the sound that the machine was detecting. The first time through, I didn't know what I was hearing, but three replays later I closed my eyes and heard the loud report of the gun I'd shot, followed a millisecond later by a muffled noise. I played the sound over and over. I was convinced the second sound was that of a .45. I listened several times before I picked it up, but after that, I heard it every time, occurring a millisecond after my initial shot with the sniper rifle. I slowly nodded. "There's something there."

I bent over the graph paper with the oscilloscope readings on it. Only the recordings made within ten feet of the man killed picked up the second shot. One, at eight feet away, showed a flicker, but the three within five feet showed positive inflections on the oscilloscope.

"That's big," Elizabeth said.

Again I played the signal of the recorder closest to the man I shot. As I tuned out the background noise to better hear that second shot, I definitely began to hear something.

After ten minutes of listening, I looked at her and said, "There's clearly a second shot in there."

The Encryption Game

I gave the headphones to Josh. He listened for a moment, then said, "Give me twelve hours and I'll have the word from my experts. But don't let any of your data get back to the prosecution. This is the sort of evidence we save until the judge demands we turn it over."

"Oh my God. Scott," Keyes said. I'm sorry I doubted you. This is brilliant."

"Look how weak the recordings of the second shot are, even on the recorders that did pick up the sound. If that was a .45, it should have been twice as loud as the sniper rifle, but here, it's so quiet, even some of the recorders didn't hear it." I looked at Josh. "Can we use that at the trial?"

"We'll see. We need to get some experts on this."

Josh stood up and looked Willis right in the eye: "There is some real conspiratorial bullshit going on around here and I'm going straight to Judge Michaels. And I assure you: She doesn't fuck around..."

Chapter 30

The Conference Room
West Wing of The White House
Washington, D.C.
11:31 a.m.

OVER THE YEARS, THE Conference Room had taken on a lot of names, The Tank, The Situation Room, The Woodshed, but for the real insiders it remained "The Conference Room," if for no other reason than if one of the senior members of the government said something to the effect of "we're meeting in The Conference Room," the others needed no translation. So when Roy Perkins called the Director of National Intelligence and said that he wanted to have an audience with the President in The Conference

Room, there was no reason to ask which one.

Perkins entered this hallowed place, the "Woodshed," with a feeling of dread. The meeting had already started to fill with the heads of the departments, or their deputies, by the time he got there. No one stood or greeted him, which was the customary courtesy given to an officer of Perkins' prestige. Only General Daniel Meyers, the Chairman of The Joint Chiefs of Staff, gave a slight head nod as Perkins quickly tested his PowerPoint presentation.

Perkins' hands were shaking. Rather than taking a seat, he stood by the viewing screen and waited, nervously.

Bart Walker, the President's National Security Advisor, took his seat close to the head of the narrow table in the center. Only one seat was vacant, that of the President's, at the end of the table. Half of the twenty or so chairs surrounding the perimeter of the room were filled with assistants and deputies. No introductions were made as Walker began the meeting. "General Perkins. We would like you to give a little background while we're waiting for the President."

The Chairman of the Joint Chiefs of Staff interrupted. "This is the business of the military courts. I object to bringing our dirty laundry to the attention of the National Security Council, the members of the cabinet, and even the President, who is not even interested in the matter."

The Vice President spoke, "I disagree with your remark. I have been made privy to the details to be presented and I feel this matter needs input from all of you, and regarding the President, he was briefed at the same time as I and he will be present after his telephone conference, within a very few minutes."

Walker continued, "All of you have a hard copy of the charges made against General Perkins, but the information I've asked him to present today has much greater importance to our national security than any misconduct issue. The President himself feels that General Perkins is the best one to show his evidence, evidence that demands immediate action, action that may prevent a terrorist attack in this country."

The Joint Chiefs Chairman looked at the Vice President with a deep, probing curiosity.

Vice President Shelly nodded at him and whispered, "Just listen. It'll knock your socks off."

The door at the opposite end of the room bolted open and the President, with his press secretary, Smith Wiggins, and Chief of Staff, Martha Eldridge, entered. The President took his chair and immediately spoke in a hurried tone. "Let's have Perkins present his evidence and I'll ask all of you to make a call on what we should do."

Perkins, using a remote, advanced the first image of the PowerPoint presentation. "Let me read this for all to hear. The first communication is a letter written by Lt. Moss to her collaborator: 'I am having a great deal of difficulty distracting General Perkins from his work. I approached him, sans bra, and leaned over in front of him, baring my breasts. He turned and walked from the room. I kissed him three times and every time, he shoved me away, once falling against the wall as he left his office.'"

Perkins advanced the image and read again: "And the reply from her confidant: 'Be more subtle in your advances. I have enjoyed your luscious body many times and know he can't resist for long. Screw him once and he's yours, like you did to me. I can't wait for you to dump him so you can return to my bed.'"

Meyers stood. He clasped his hands behind his back and slowly walked along the table until he arrived at the viewing screen and looked it over. He cleared his throat and turned to Perkins. "I just can't believe your words. You'll have to share any evidence that supports your contention. And the same is true for the sexual battery charges. I have to be honest here, Roy: It seems to me that you're trying to slander the young woman that you, you, whatever...Just to discredit her. I can look the other way on a lot of things. But I am sick and tired of seeing people in powerful positions using those powerful positions for perverted means. Catholic priests. Football coaches. Congressmen. I'm sick of it. If you have used your authority to intimidate that poor girl into having sex with you, or if you forced yourself on her, then I assure you, I am no longer your friend."

"Dan," Perkins said, visibly shaken by the Chairman's lecture, "she was working with someone."

"So?" the Chairman of the Joint Chiefs interjected. "So you're being extorted from. So?"

The Secretary of Defense shifted in his chair. "Is this smut any of our business?" He openly laughed as he said, "Better not let Fox get this story. They'll accuse the Democrats of doing porno in our meetings."

The President spoke quickly, "Just listen a moment, Dan. And hurry along General Perkins."

"There's more. I am accused of divulging United States classified material, specifically the specifications of the 'behind the wall grenades' that are being developed in

The Encryption Game

Picatinny Arsenal in New Jersey." Perkins hit the remote and a series of diagrams showed the details of the circuits of the electronic detectors embedded in the grenades. After the grenade was shot and was itself "behind the wall," a chip inside the grenade enabled the explosive to wait until it recognized the enemy combatant before initiating detonation. No further signal was required from the one who fired the grenade. If there were no enemy there, the ordinance didn't explode and was operational for a later opportunity. This was considered a breakthrough-type weapon by many in anti-terrorism. "This is all so highly classified that only a few at the Pentagon know about this. I did not give these to Lt. Moss. These documents and plans didn't originate with me. I saw these same pages only once before, in a PowerPoint demonstration at a single Pentagon briefing. But I never had these documents in my hands, nor did I ever have access to them. These pages were mailed to Moss from an inside informant."

Perkins advanced another image and read: " 'We have delayed the exposure of this material until it will benefit us most. Now is the time. This will discredit General Perkins and distract the Pentagon's attention from our activities.' "

Chairman Meyers frowned as he looked at Perkins. "Prove that these documents are legitimate!"

"I don't have the absolute proof because that exists in only two places, the computer of Lt. Moss, which I have never had access to, and the computer of her informant."

"Obviously, you're telling me you gained this material from a hacker. Your lawyer should be well aware that this kind of evidence is not allowable under court protocol."

"I'm not talking about my trial! Gentlemen, Mr.

President: We have a mole employed in a high position in the Pentagon. I'm sure of it. We're in trouble. We have to move quickly."

The President waved his hand in a circle. "Come on, come on. We know who these people are. Let's get on with the show. General Perkins."

"You are correct, Mr. President." Perkins took a deep breath before saying, loud and clear: "Master Sergeant Assam Jassak is the informant. His and Lt. Moss' computers contain all the information I've presented about the charges."

A confusion broke out in the room, combined with a lot of mumblings and clearing of throats.

Secretary Carter answered, "I have reviewed General Perkins' assertions and they are correct. And your next question to General Perkins will open a huge kettle of worms, one that will be of extreme concern to all of you, as well as our nation as a whole: Do we allow this evidence to be released to the public?"

The President himself stood and spoke: "I'll take the responsibility for this. Court Orders for the search of this man's residence and that of Lt. Moss will be obtained immediately, before these two do more harm. If this thing plays out as you say, then you will be exonerated of the battery charges, General Perkins. What the Department of Defense will have to say about the fact that you didn't notify your superior about Lt. Moss' improper advances is another matter." The President, a little exasperated, nodded to his Chief of Staff, Eldridge. "Just move it along. Move it along!"

Chapter 31

The Pentagon
Washington, D.C.
12:31 p.m.

OFFICERS FROM THE PENTAGON'S police force, the Pentagon Force Protection Agency, met, quietly, with agents from the FBI and the CIA, to discuss a plan that they were informally calling "Operation Mr. Clean," the hurriedly put-together scheme designed to capture the computers and files of Moss and Jassak. Surprise was paramount. It was agreed that any sign of law enforcement should be hidden. Nothing official, no badges, nothing. It was decided that two Marine officers should be called in. This was the Pentagon, no one would expect them to be making an arrest. The two Marines were given simple instructions. They were told to "get those people away from their computers as fast as possible by whatever means necessary," and "don't let their hands touch that keyboard once they know what's happening—just yank'em away and tackle'em—we'll do the rest."

With law enforcement officials waiting quietly in the hallway, the two Marine captains approached Moss' desk, smiling, just like they were told. One of them held out his hand and said, "Lt. Moss, I'm so glad to meet you." Moss looked up from her computer and stood, offering her hand. It was the perfect opportunity, too good to waste. The Marine grabbed the outstretched hand and attempted to twist it behind her back.

Moss was no Air Force Lieutenant. She was, in fact, a carefully trained operative. This, apparently, hadn't been taken into consideration during the hastily thrown together "Mr. Clean." Her lightning-fast kick to the captain's shin activated a spring-loaded blade in the toe of her shoe. It penetrated deeply into his shin. He spontaneously shouted in pain and surprise and loosened his grip. Moss tore her arm loose and reached in her bra, coming out with a knife, and then spun around to thrust it into his throat. The stunned captain grabbed his neck and dropped to one knee, his eyes already dimming. The other captain's jaw dropped. *What the...? This was supposed to be an easy deal!* He jumped to the side and swung hard at Moss's face. She dodged, trapped his wrist in mid-swing, and, using both arms, slung him to the floor, dropped to one knee, and shoved her knife under his ribs and into his heart.

The other office workers sat frozen by the sudden and intense fight. "Oh my God!" the receptionist shouted. "Call security!"

The Encryption Game

At long last, Second Lieutenant Mark Hawley, a diminutive Special Forces flunkey who despised his desk job and who sat two places behind Moss, had his chance to *do something*. Soldiers a lot bigger than he had stair-stepped over him to gain promotion. But seeing that Moss was not at all what everybody thought she was, he saw his opportunity to prove himself.

Others may be stronger, but his asset was quickness. With cat-like speed, he sprang from his chair, vaulted over the desk in front of him, and grabbed Moss' wrist. He immediately turned the blade toward her and kept moving. His forward momentum took her down by surprise and pushed the blade deep into her chest. They crashed hard to the floor. He relaxed, momentarily, thinking that he'd done it—he'd taken down the threat. But the wounded terrorist reached again into her bra. Lt. Hawley clamped down on her chest with both of his hands. He could feel her fingers move inside the bra. He felt a thumb-sized metallic object, and lifted his weight from her to grab what looked like a bomb trigger. She shoved his body away and lurched for the trigger. His hand grabbed it just a split second before hers. She grabbed and twisted his hand, but he held on tightly. She struggled to take it from him, but was weak from internal blood loss. She gasped twice, then was still.

The Pentagon Force Protection guys burst in from the hallway, belatedly, to carry away Moss' computers, as well as the contents of her desk.

It had not gone well, to say the least. The hastily thrown together "Mr. Clean" had been a fiasco.

Defense Munitions Inventory Control
The Pentagon
2:00 p.m.

JASSAK'S PHONE RANG. He picked up and heard a secretary say, "Sergeant, please report to Colonel Jacob's office. And bring the Boeing contract."

Jassak took the file and walked down the hall to his superior's office. As he approached, he saw the door open very slightly. His hair bristled on his neck. He backed away, then turned and ran to his desk. Opening the locked bottom drawer, he took out a heavy object and stuffed it in his pocket. Returning to the suspicious door, he pushed softly, saw someone or something waiting for him, then shoved the door open hard against the voyeur, knocking him against the wall. Suddenly the door to Colonel Jacob's office flew open and four men dressed in SWAT gear stormed out. Jassak had trained for this in Pakistan. He withdrew his snub-nosed .38 pistol and fired above the sternal body armor, placing his four shots in each of their necks.

There was thunder in the hallway as ten SWAT officers swarmed the room. After Moss, there would be no more attempts at finesse. Automatic fire from three M-16s cut him down.

Chapter 32

Islander Burgers Restaurant
Quantico, Virginia
11:01 p.m.

THE ARGUMENT STARTED BECAUSE Special Agent Hopkins, our "minder," wouldn't let me take my kids to dinner. I wanted to get out of the Marine base and take my family to get a burger. Yes, we were under protective custody. Yes, I understood that Farok and maybe others were looking for me. But it seemed crazy to have a family night out without my family.

I had made the request in the morning, and throughout the day Agent Hopkins had been talking to her superiors about getting some extra protection for us, and about dealing with the press and the media. I really just wanted to get out of the confining, regimented atmosphere of the base, and have a little normal, family-time with my boys. At the end of a gigantic hassle, the decision was made to allow Keyes and me to leave the base for dinner, with Hopkins as our guard, but the kids had to stay at the FBI dorm with Mom. Even then, we were told, we'd have to leave carefully, quietly, and not tell anyone of our whereabouts or plans. The FBI seemed to be more worried about a press leak and a media circus than security against terrorists.

There was even an argument in the car about where to go. Without the kids, it seemed crazy to go to Islander Burgers, but then again going to some quiet little candle-lit place with Agent Hopkins didn't seem very pleasant, either. By the time we walked into the restaurant, Hopkins and Keyes weren't even speaking to each other. I texted Jakjak and told him where to meet us, hoping that his presence would break up the tension, even though I knew that Hopkins and her friends were going to be upset.

After a tumultuous two weeks of events, the conventional environment of your average mid-range family restaurant brightened my mood. It was late and people were slowly trickling out and going home. Two young women sat at the bar. Most of the others looked like government employees, IT people, clerks, with several wearing their Quantico credentials on strings around their necks, and dressed professionally. We were greeted by a young girl, perhaps no more than sixteen or seventeen, who was bright and sunny. A television hung in the corner, over the bar, with the news running, going back and forth to a shot of a ballgame that had just ended and a couple

The Encryption Game

of sportscasters. There was some chatter—a mildly loud crowd. It was nice. On one side of the place, waitresses were cleaning up after a large party.

I looked for Jakjak, but I didn't see him. I didn't care what the FBI thought, I really missed hanging around with the big fella.

We sat at the bar and I had a moment to think about what my life had become. Everything was a struggle now. I was thankful that I had Josh Edwards on my side. I didn't want to feel paranoid, but it was hard. I felt myself worrying about going to the bathroom, worrying about what was on the other side of every corner. I worried about how far a possible conspiracy against me could go. I worried about that freak who'd come to my jail cell on the second day. Hearing from Jakjak had relieved me immensely. Apparently that weird guy wasn't a hallucination. That helped.

I ordered a cheeseburger with everything on it, and double fries. And a good whiskey. And another good whiskey. Neither Keyes nor Agent Hopkins ordered. Suddenly they'd lost their appetite, and that depressed things. My attempt at normalcy wasn't working out. When Jakjak got there I was sure that Hopkins would have some choice words about my violation of her edict that no one was supposed to know where we'd gone.

Then it all went out the window, so to speak. Keyes blurted, "Oh no! Oh my God, no!"

I jumped, then recovered and looked at the television. Keyes threw her hand over her mouth. "Oh my God, Scott, no…"

Scrolling across the bottom of the screen, in small

white letters against the black tape, were the words, "Defense lawyer for accused capital murder suspect Scott James killed in hit and run. Attorney, Josh Edwards, 31, was pronounced dead at the scene."

"Oh God," I groaned. I stood and walked toward the TV, to get a better look, but the news of Josh's death had already rolled by. I felt a wave of dread flood over me. There was simply no way that this was an accident, just no way.

"No... No... No..." Keyes was murmuring, her voice cracking.

My heart hurt, and I grasped the bar with one hand and turned to look at her. Hopkins was busy texting, obviously trying to get confirmation of the death. Looking back toward Keyes, I saw the double doors of the restaurant open to reveal two men. They were both thin, probably in their early twenties, wearing baggy clothing and black vests with ammo magazines in the pockets. They both carried old, worn, AK-47s.

"KEYES!! LOOKOUT!!"

Both gunmen looked at me. They had me cold. This was how it would end. I'd escaped so much, come so far, and now, finally, this was it. They raised their rifles, took aim, and then a muscular black arm came over the head of one of the gunman and I heard a gigantic, deep-throated roar, like a lion in the distance, "WWWHAAAAAAAAAAGHHHH!"

Jakjak.

The gunman's head snapped backward just as he opened fire. The rifle fired four quick shots, *BOOM BOOM BOOM BOOM,* shattering ceiling tiles and randomly spraying death as the barrel of the weapon whipped in the wide arc of the man's body being bent back. Going down with his man's neck firmly locked in the crook of his arm, Jakjak lifted his leg at the last second and planted his heel in the other gunman's hip and kicked hard. The second gunman's body twisted from the impact and he fell, firing wildly. Glass exploded all around us. Bullets blew out light bulbs and shattered the windows in the entrance area. The young girl who had seated us screamed a shrill, "OWWW-MY-GAAAWWD!" Hopkins bolted from her seat, drew her pistol, and emptied the entire magazine in a well-controlled, nine-round burst. We saw the second gunman's head slam backward from the shells, his neck jumping and falling from the concussion of the bullets. Jakjak struggled wildly with the first gunman. Hopkins took off running for the man and then we saw him raise the rifle with his one free hand and fire a long series of desperation shots. Hopkins dropped like a rag doll, face down, with blood gushing onto the floor all around her. The mirror behind the bar shattered. Tables toppled over and chairs squealed across the floors as the restaurant emptied of people, terrified and running. He kept firing and firing as Jakjak strangled the life out of him.

And then it was silent. A dense cloud of gun smoke hung on everything. The smell of sulfur was intense. I hesitated. I waited for the blast of the suicide vest that must surely come.

Keyes stood up and shouted, "Get away! He'll detonate his vest!"

But nothing happened. There was no explosion. There'd been no suicide vest on the two who had followed

Jakjak on the previous day, either. I was relieved, but it also gave me a sense of fear, too. What was this? I looked in every direction, scanning for the second team that must surely be there. "Jakjak!" I yelled, "Jakjak! Are you okay?"

"I am fine, Dokte! But watch for de udda team! De wheel be mor-ah!"

"Elizabeth! Are you hit?"

"No! But she is!"

I ran to Hopkins, turned her over, and felt my heart sink. She was quite dead. The profuse bleeding had already started to slow to a steady drain. Her heart made no sounds. She had at least four holes in her upper chest and neck.

"Dokte! We got ta get outta hee-a! Dokte! Let's go! Run!"

"Scott!" Keyes said, "We've got to go! We've got to get out of here!"

Keyes strode over to the dead gunmen and quickly and methodically stripped them of their weapons and ammo, then turned to me and said, "Come on, Scott! Let's get out of here!"

I took one last look at the dead FBI agent, and ran.

We burst through the doors of the restaurant and followed Jakjak to the car.

The black Evora was so small and so low to the ground that I instinctively tried to put Keyes in the back seat, but she said, "No! *You* get back there! I'm driving!"

At that particular moment, I really didn't feel like discussing the finer points of the travel arrangements, so I dove in, pulled the seat back, and Jakjak got in front. We could hear the sirens in the distance. "That's the cops!" I said, "Let's just go around the block and come back. After they're here, we're good!"

"No fucking way!" Keyes shouted.

The motor raced as soon as she turned the key over. She put the car in gear and then that aggressive engine roared and I was suddenly flattened against the backseat by the g-forces. The Lotus took off with the tires squealing. We lurched hard through the first turn out of the parking lot and I found myself clawing wildly at the soft leather interior, trying to stay upright.

Chapter 33

Day 17
Elkins Regional Airport
Elkins, West Virginia
Hangar D
1:00 a.m.

THE NIGHT WATCHMAN HAD maintained his distance from Hangar D because the balloonists had made it clear to his boss, Larry Waltrip, that they wanted privacy. But when the hangar doors cracked opened at around midnight, the elderly security guard drove his old truck toward the activity and parked behind the adjacent hangar.

He sat in his old pick-up, observing Hangar D through his binoculars. The people inside the hangar were clearly getting a weird-looking contraption ready for flight. The elderly watchman had seen a lot of different aircraft at

Waltrip's airport over the years, but this thing was very strange. He looked through the hangar doors now at an extremely long plastic tube, with what looked like a space capsule attached to one end. He immediately phoned Waltrip, whom he woke out of a sound sleep. "Boss, something funny's going on—something with those guys in Hangar D. Something's not right. You'd better check it out."

"Okay. I'll come down," Waltrip said, groggily, and then hung up.

The passenger-side door of the old truck jerked open. The old man turned to see what was happening. He felt the barrel of a gun against his head. As it discharged, he felt nothing as he tumbled through space.

1:20 a.m.

WALTRIP WAS QUICKLY AT the airport. It was very dark out, the only light being the glow coming from the partially opened doors of Hangar D. He parked next to his watchman's old truck, got out, then opened the driver's side door. His man tumbled out, into his arms. Before he could react, four strong hands grabbed him, jerked him backward, threw a sack over his face, and bound his arms and legs in duct tape.

They carried the squirming Waltrip directly to Hangar D. There, a tall black man snatched the bag from his head and spoke abruptly: "You are the owner, are you not?"

"What the hell is going on here?"

"Cooperate, and you live. Give me a hard time, and you die. You are in aviation administration. You know about radar on the east coast, correct? You also know about the emergency systems, the locations of the beacons, the towers, everything. Right?"

What the terrorists didn't know was that Larry Waltrip was now in his element. He had the home field advantage. He'd been a Prisoner of War, a POW in Viet Nam, and he knew what to do. He'd stall for time, for his life. He'd lie. Then maybe he'd escape. "Yes," he said, measuring the terrorists that now surrounded him. "I know everything you need to know about that."

The terrorist leader smiled and turned to one of his men. "Let him live until you meet up with the other guys. Send a message to the Emir. We now have a fountain of knowledge after the Internet is down."

Inside, Waltrip shivered at the implications, but outward he showed nothing. They were going to use him, there was no way around that.

They wrapped roll after roll of two-inch tape around his arms, legs, and mouth, then carried him to a stack of cardboard boxes and pitched him in. He tried to move, but the tape was secure. Movement of any kind was a joke. A cold sweat covered his body.

2:50 a.m.

SVEN MOBRIS, THE FATHER of the balloon, proudly directed the men in preparing for launch. To help with the lift-off, Omar had sent in ten of his best soldiers, all of who seemed to understand basic operations, electronics, and how to work as a team.

The light inside the hangar was bad, and outside it was

pitch black. Each man wore his own six-volt headlamp for extra illumination. Mobris, standing front and center, directed the jaws of a forklift to carefully grasp the flimsy balloon and pull it outside. Wheeled dollies supported other segments of the giant plastic tube to keep it from dragging on the asphalt. A separate forklift carried the attached capsule in a synchronized transport of the entire flimsy aircraft.

Mobris directed the careful movement of the high-altitude balloon to the center of the main runway, a hundred yards from the hangar. The blond Swedish designer continuously barked orders. After a moment, a truck pulled out of the hangar, filled with Helium canisters, and cruised over to park beside the capsule.

Mobris looked at his watch. "It's crazy to launch so early in the morning. It's so much easier in the daylight."

The tall threatening man who had supervised the killing of the night watchman and the interrogation of Larry Waltrip, stated, "If you want your bonus, the balloon needs to take flight before six."

Chapter 34

Somewhere On Highway 66
Virginia
3:54 a.m.

WE PULLED OVER IN the dark, and got out to stretch our legs. I looked at Elizabeth and Jakjak and said, "I have to call my kids and tell them everything is alright."

"Use my phone," Keyes said. "I've deactivated the GPS. They're still going to be able to find us, but not immediately."

She pitched me her phone, and I dialed Mom.

Obviously, she'd been up all night. "Scott?" she said on the other end of the line, "What happened? The authorities have been swarming the place. They told me to contact them the moment I heard from you."

199

"I understand. Put Scotty on the phone."

"What?"

"I want to talk to my boy. Please. Hurry."

I waited, knowing it would only be a matter of time before they would triangulate my position.

Scotty picked up the phone, obviously half asleep. I had to make it short. "Scotty, I want you to know that I love you and I want you to always know that your Dad is innocent."

"I know that. Are you hurt? When are you and Elizabeth coming back?"

"I don't know."

"Is Special Agent Hopkins with you? They said she was hurt."

"No, Buddy, she's ... She's not with us."

"Is Jakjak there?"

"Yes."

"Tell Elizabeth that I'm getting really good at encryption—or *de*cryption. She wants me to know the difference."

"I'll tell her."

"I looked at her stuff. It was laying out."

"What stuff?"

"Her encryption game. It was left out. I wasn't snooping. It was out."

"That's okay, Buddy. Don't worry about it."

"Tell her I got it. It's 'balloon', and 'elk'."

"I'll tell her, Buddy. But I think it's 'missile', and 'emp'."

"No! Dad! Not all of them! She didn't know! She said they were all the same, but some say 'balloon', and 'elk'.

The Encryption Game

Dad! I got it! You just have to look at the double letters. Balloon has two sets of double letters, missile only has one set. That's how I figured it out. There are only a few seven-lettered words that have two sets of double letters. After that, I knew what L was, and I figured out what E was. Some are 'emp' but there is only one three-lettered word that these other ones could be, 'elk'."

"Okay. Okay, Buddy. I'll tell her. I have to go now. Tell Jeremy and Mom that I love them both. I don't think I'll be back for a long time. I'm sorry."

My son began to cry.

"I love you, Scotty. I have to go."

With that, I hung up.

"Scott," Keyes said, softly. "I'm sorry."

"What do you suggest we do now?"

She drew a deep breath. "Hide. Or...I don't know. Maybe we should go to the news media. Or maybe Perkins. One way or another, I don't think you should trust the authorities. Either way, we have to move away from this position immediately. Even without GPS, they'll be able to locate where you called from."

"The media? God, they think I'm a nut. They twist everything I say. The minute I shot that guy I became 'part of the problem' in their eyes. God, I can't go back to jail. I don't have a lawyer. I don't have anything. I'm the guiltiest man in America as far as this country is concerned. Perkins is compromised, which means he's not much use anymore. He was the only one who knew the truth about me. Also, that guy—the guy who came to my cell—he said to keep quiet and he'd protect me."

"Dokte: Dees guy ees very weird. Forget heem."

201

"I don't know. I have a feeling that he may really be on my side."

"Scott," Keyes said in a frank but caring tone, "don't mention him to anyone. You already appear crazy. If you start talking about a secret man, they're going to think you're like Son of Sam or something."

I thought about my dwindling options. Everything looked bad. I drew a deep breath and let it out slowly. "I do have some good news, though: Scotty says he beat you at the encryption game. He says your decryption is wrong. He says some of the words that you thought were repeats aren't repeats. They're not 'missile' and 'emp'. Some of them are 'balloon' and 'elk'. So ..." I smiled, as best as I could, "You'll have to argue with him on that."

"What?"

I thought of my son's face. He was going to grow up to be one smart guy—but the son of a famous killer.

"He went through my notes?"

"He says you left them out. You've created a monster. He's going to be one of those people who see code words and ciphers in everything. He said that because there were two sets of double letters in 'balloon' and only one set in 'missile', that it had to be 'balloon'. He figured out the rest from there. You'll have to straighten him out on that some day."

Keyes stared at me.

"Come on. He's a good kid. He just thought it was a game. He didn't hurt anything. You know, my kids still think you're Dad's office manager. They don't know you're involved in ... whatever."

Keyes started walking around in a circle, with her head

The Encryption Game

down. "Balloon... Balloon ..."

"Don't worry about it. I told him there was no way that it could be the solution. I'm sure your reputation will survive. Let's get moving. I would imagine they're tracking us in some fashion. The only thing we have on our side is our own random movements."

Keyes' face went pale. "He's going to attack with a balloon."

"What?"

"A balloon. Farok is using a balloon."

"And an elk. Farok is going to attack with an elk. So ... that'll be interesting."

"Scott! Farok is just the type of guy who would use a fucking balloon! He'd—"

"What are you talking about? That's just nomenclature! Like 'wedding' or 'eggplant'—"

"No! It's not!"

"What? How can you know?"

"Because, Scott, for an EMP to work, the bomb has to explode at high-altitude. There are only two ways to get to the stratosphere: by rocket, or by high-altitude balloon. A missile gets you noticed. It's hard to hide. If you get stopped somewhere along the line, you're fried—you've got a *missile* in your truck. They're big. They look like missiles. Also, you've got to either build the thing or obtain it. But a balloon is nothing. You can build one in your shop. It's *civilian*. It's just a big clump of plastic. If you get stopped with a balloon in your truck, nobody cares."

"What happens if you get stopped with an elk in your truck?"

Jakjak started smiling. "Dokte..." he said, laughing at my lame joke. "You should be more generous with Mademoiselle. But that was a good one."

"Scott," she said, shaking her head. "Let me tell you something about being an operative, something that has saved my life many times: Expect the unexpected."

"I'm going to turn myself in. I'll take my chances. If I keep running, I just look more guilty. Game over."

Keyes started walking in circles again, working her cell phone.

"Who are you calling?" I asked.

No answer.

I stepped over and looked over her shoulder. She was typing out "balloon," "Gettysburg address," and "elk," on Google. The search came up. Keyes looked at the listings. Nothing. She selected the second page. Nothing. She selected the third. The first line said, "Come to Elkins Airport for all your ballooning needs."

"Oh, shit," I said.

Keyes tapped the screen and a website for Elkins Airport came up. In bright blue letters it said, "Elkins provides all you need. Ballast. Ballast bags. Tie downs. Extra hangar space. Meteorological support. Chase vehicles. Come to Elkins! See the Civil War battlefields from the air! We're Balloon Friendly!"

"There is no way," I whispered.

"Someday you're going to trust me."

"I'm calling the cops."

"The hell you are, Scott. We're going to Elkins right now. It's an hour away."

"Eh ..."

The Encryption Game

"It's four o'clock in the morning, Scott. What are you going to tell the cops? 'Hi guys! Doctor Scott James here. I'm the guy you know from TV. I'm the Lee Harvey Oswald wannabe. By the way, a terrorist acquaintance of mine has a live nuke right down the road at your little municipal airport. And it's gonna be launched from a *balloon*. Oh, and in case you're wondering, I haven't been drinking.'"

"Well, I'm at least going to call Perkins."

"Why don't you call him when we get there. You can wait an hour to commit suicide, right? Because I don't want to be around when you tell him that little Scotty, Champion of Celebrity Ciphers, just broke a terrorist code and now you think that Perkins, who's under indictment, should call out the Marines to stage an assault on little Elkins Airport."

I chuckled grimly "I'll buy that. An hour isn't gonna make much difference in the grand scheme of my ultimate demise."

"I'm driving."

Chapter 35

Runway 23/5
Elkins Regional Airport
5:00 a.m.

THE FILLING OF THE balloon was complete. Above the capsule there floated a giant plastic bubble of helium, enough gas to take the capsule to the stratosphere.

Mobris directed the last-minute preparations for launch. He leaned over the shoulder of his only technician, worrying and watching every little detail. He knew that the man knew the precise settings and connections, but his compulsive nature wouldn't allow him to stand by and direct from a distance.

"Do you wish to check my program?" the tech asked.

Without answering, Mobris moved the man aside and

fiddled with the controls — without making any changes. He went over everything once more. He checked the pressurized hatch to make sure it closed correctly. "Perfect," he said. He made sure the on-board oxygen systems were ready. He stood and looked over the connecting harness that went from the top of the capsule to the balloon. Finally, he shook his head. "We're on schedule to meet the deadline, but it's crazy."

A forklift came rolling out from the hangar with a shiny silver cylinder resting on its jaws. The North Koreans had removed all traces of Korean writing and had put a combination of British, Israeli, and Russian lettering on the warhead to make it look like it had been made from spare parts. They had entirely succeeded in fooling all those working on the project into believing that Farok had somehow managed to build his own nuke from odds and ends, which he claimed he'd acquired on the world's black markets.

The special warhead that the Koreans were so proud of wasn't exactly as compact and refined as an American W-80. It weighed roughly 490 pounds and was encased in lead. As the forklift got into position, Mobris called over all of the biggest guys to help. They gathered around and hoisted the cylinder off the forklift, their muscles straining, and placed the bomb in its cradle, at the back of the capsule.

At last, everything was in place. For the past week they'd worked through one checklist after another to get to this point. All the details were done. All they needed now was the pilot, and they could launch.

Chapter 36

Highway 33
Ten Miles From Elkins Regional Airport
5:04 a.m.

KEYES WAS ALMOST OUT of control. She was driving the Lotus like a wild woman. The engine, located right behind the back seat, was so loud that my ears were ringing. At the highway turn off, she shouted, "HOLD ON!" and we swerved through the interchange with the tires roaring on the cement.

Operations Command
Somewhere on the Virginia Coast
5:15 a.m.

AT A CROWDED, SMOKE-FILLED apartment, they waited anxiously for word from Emir Farok.

At last, the signal came:

Go to your assigned positions. We are GO.

The game was on. All the operatives on the eastern seaboard knew that "assigned positions" meant "underground." That was all they knew, but it didn't take a genius to figure out that a big weapon was about to be released, one that would make being above ground unsurvivable.

Chapter 37

Taxiway
Elkins Regional Airport
5:20 a.m.

THE TIME HAD COME. From the hangar doors, the pilot of the balloon emerged and began to walk stiffly and laboriously toward the waiting capsule. He wore a white and blue pressure suit, for high-altitude, with his head and face completely covered by a helmet and visor. From his chest, an oxygen hose snaked down from a portal, around his upper torso, and plugged into the wide, flat container on the back of his suit. Three men wearing backpacks followed him.

The walk of only one hundred yards took two full

minutes due to the difficulties of moving in the heavy pressure suit. By the time he reached the capsule, it was clear that the pilot was breathing heavily. At the capsule, he said to Mobris, through his visor, "Are we ready for lift off?"

Mobris looked at the balloon, with its long, skinny body and helium bubble at the top, and said, "We're ready. But we're not flying just yet. As soon as you give me the money Emir Farok promised, with my bonus for meeting his 6:00 a.m. deadline, I'll wish you 'bon voyage.'"

The pilot stood there stoically for a moment, then turned to the three men who'd followed him from the hangar. The backpacks that they wore were obviously very heavy. They had to lean over against the weight just to stand. The pilot tried to snap his fingers in the tight-fitting space gloves of the pressure suit, but was unsuccessful. It didn't matter to the three men. They knew what to do. They flung the backpacks off, one by one, each of which hit the ground with a loud *carump*.

The pilot turned to Mobris and said though his visor, "It's all there. A million dollars weighs twenty-one pounds. The twenty million is there, as well as the ten million bonus, over 185 pounds of bills."

Mobris smiled. This is just what he'd asked for, more or less. He wanted cash, big piles of it, just like a big drug deal—instant gratification, and completely untraceable, random.

The pilot entered the craft and took his seat, and Mobris closed the hatch. The father of the balloon was very proud at this moment. His invention, his brilliance, was about to take flight. He would see the balloon lift off, and then

The Encryption Game

he'd head underground. He would have almost two hours before the bomb went off. Plenty of time.

With the hatch closed, Mobris stepped back and looked around for a moment. All clear. The only thing left to do now was to release the straining contraption from its bonds.

There were five restraining lines attached to capsule. Each of these ran down to a fifty-pound bag of lead shot. Before the bomb had been loaded on, there had been twenty of these anchor-bags holding down the big swollen helium bubble. These five were the last.

Mobris reached up and pulled the pin from the shackle on the first line, and it fell away. He signaled to his jump-suited technician on the other side of the capsule to release the second line. The tech pulled the pin out and the line fell. The tech then released a third line, then Mobris released the fourth. The balloon began to lift off. Mobris shouted, "No! No! The last line!"

They both leaped for the quick-release pin, but it was too late. The capsule was eight feet off the ground and beyond reach. The bag of shot still hung over the side. It weighed just enough to slow the balloon down, but not enough to stop it. Mobris pulled his work knife out of his pocket and lunged at the bag of shot, nipping a corner of the fabric. Lead pellets streamed out onto the runway as the balloon climbed out of reach for good. Slowly but surely the capsule was rising, and the excess lead was leaking out.

Finally, it was airborne. Mobris smiled as the balloon lifted slowly away. The line still hung down, but at least the shot would eventually all pour out.

Mobris watched the first hundred feet of the flight, then snapped out of his trance. He noticed that all of Farok's men were staring at him. Maybe they wanted money. He hurriedly grabbed the backpacks together in a pile and then unzipped the top of one to have a look.

Inside, he found rectangles of blank paper. He pulled out handfuls of them, allowing them to spill out on the cement. He couldn't believe it. Then he turned and looked into the barrel of a .45. The last thing Mobris saw was the first flash of two gunshots.

Chapter 38

Highway 33
Elkins, West Virginia
5:30 a.m.

I COULD SEE THE halo of sunshine as dawn approached. On the near horizon, I looked and saw a long, spindly object floating in complete daylight. The sun was glinting off of the balloon-and-capsule. It was slowly ascending into the dawn.

Jakjak called out, "*Dokte!* The balloon!"

"Oh my God, Scott," Keyes shouted over the racing engine, "They've already launched!"

The only balloons I'd ever seen before were perfectly round, brightly colored, and had people in wicker baskets a few feet below. This thing must have been a hundred feet tall, with a fat, oval, twenty-foot expansion at the top, like a pregnant snake. Bundles of cables dropped to a solid, egg-shaped structure, about eight feet in diameter. "Sure doesn't look like it's much of an aircraft," I said.

"That's the way high-altitude balloons look as they're going up," Keyes said, desperately. "The helium expands as the atmospheric pressure drops. By the time they reach 100,000 feet, the pressure is way down, and all that hanging plastic will expand to be as round as a beach ball."

The capsule was only about a hundred feet in the air, and rising ever so slowly in the dim gray light of the early dawn.

Keyes turned sharply and drove into the airport. We heard a gunshot, a distant pop, and then a second one. As we reached the taxiway and the view opened up, we saw a group of eight men walking toward the hangars and two bodies lying on the cement.

Keyes eyes narrowed, "Farok..."

Chapter 39

Elkins Regional Airport
5:41 a.m.

KEYES REACHED BEHIND THE seat and pulled out a blood-spattered AK-47. She shifted gear, clicked off the safety of the gun, then stomped on the accelerator, heading right for the group of walking men. She put her right hand on the wheel, and with her left put the AK-47 out the window, resting the barrel on the side view mirror. She shouted "Fucking Farok!" and unleashed two full bursts. The noise of the gun was like a jackhammer. Hot shells came spewing out of the chamber and the car was flooded with the smell of sulfur. Keyes took a sharp right, to get a better angle, and then let go of another burst and we saw two guys go down.

The rest were running for their lives now and we could see the doors of a hangar at the far end of the airport being pushed closed. The Lotus was bucking and swerving, dodging parked cars and aircraft. The last of the running men slipped inside the far hangar just as we got there.

Keyes screeched to a stop and we piled out. We faced a real problem now: There wasn't enough sunlight yet to illuminate the inside of the hangar, and we had no idea of the size of our opposing force. "Let's make this a two-pronged attack," I said.

Jakjak drew his 9mm and ran around the side of the hangar. I heard a window break and the sound of Jakjak's gun. As Keyes and I tried to pull the hangar door open, we were met with a hail of bullets that filled the door opening. I jumped out of the way just as a man flew through the air and tackled me. At the same time, the bright hangar lights came on and I saw my attacker very clearly. His knife was raised over his head, ready to strike. I moved to the side as his blade struck next to me. I grabbed his arm and twisted. Keyes was firing into the hangar. I saw a second man running toward us with a shovel in his hand. He swung before I ducked. I was dead—but for Elizabeth's aim. I heard the loud report of her gun. The shovel struck my shoulder, but with no force. He crumpled at my side. I twisted the arm with the knife, threw the knife-wielding man off of me, and Keyes fired twice into his chest.

I called out to Jakjak, "Are they all down?"

"No! De run away! De are running out de back way!"

There was a sudden commotion at the far side of the hangar. Jakjak climbed through the shattered window and Elizabeth covered me as I jogged toward the sounds, poised to shoot.

There was a man underneath a bunch of boxes. He tried to call out, but his voice was muffled. We pointed our guns and walked quietly to him. Then, as we moved the boxes away, we saw a man, tightly bound all over—even his mouth was covered—with a huge amount of duct tape.

Elizabeth kept her aim on him as I removed the tape. He was a tall man with gray and black hair, heavily tanned skin, wrinkled from years of sun exposure, wearing casual but expensive sportswear. He held his eyebrows high to see through the loose skin in his upper lids and heavily wrinkled lowers. Even in the dim light, his green eyes were penetrating. As I freed him of the tape, he jumped to his feet and shook my hand.

"Who are you?" I asked.

Chapter 40

Hangar D
Elkins Regional Airport
5:45 a.m.

"Larry Waltrip. I'm the owner of this airport. Who the hell are you?"

Given my recent fame, I didn't want to say who I was, so I just said, "My name is Scott. What happened?"

"The guys who rented this hangar killed my security guard and took me prisoner."

"I think those same guys just launched a balloon out here on the runway."

"I figured as much," Waltrip said, and then he walked past me and out the hangar door.

We followed Waltrip out into the light, to look for

the balloon. Only a few minutes had elapsed since we'd arrived, but it was already high in the sky, just a speck, really.

"Aw-right, you sum-bitch," Waltrip grumbled. "Now I gotcha."

The old man stomped off toward the nearest hangar.

I looked at Keyes and Jakjak and said, "We've still got one ace, and that's Perkins. Maybe they can shoot it down."

"They'll never make it, Scott. Even if they believe us and even if people believe Perkins, it would take too long. It would take too many phone calls. It would take them a couple of hours, at least."

"I've still got to warn them."

I took out my phone and dialed Perkins. He answered on the first ring. "James? Where the hell are you? What happened to the FBI Agent who was with you? Someone said there was a shooting in—"

"Perkins, listen to me: Farok may have put a nuke on a balloon, a balloon which just took off from Elkins, West Virginia. I think he's going to try to do an EMP."

"Whaaaaaaaaaaat? What are you talking about? A *balloon?*"

Behind me, I could hear Waltrip loudly rolling open the clattering metal doors of a hangar.

"Perkins, listen: Keyes broke Farok's code. He's trying to launch an EMP, but instead of using a missile to shoot the nuke up into the stratosphere, he's using a high-altitude balloon to carry it up there. That balloon just took off no more than five minutes ago from this little airport out here. I saw it take off and we had a firefight with a bunch of guys who look like Farok's men."

"Oh my God!" Perkins exclaimed. "Are you *sure?*"

Suddenly Keyes pointed behind me and asked, quietly, "What's he doing?"

I turned to see Waltrip pushing an enormous blue biplane out of the hangar. It was an old Stearman, a two-seater aircraft with bright yellow wings and a thick silver propeller.

Clearly, Larry was going flying.

"Perkins. I...Eh... I'll call you back," I said, then hung up.

Waltrip began putting on a flying cap made of gray webbing, with headphones and a voice activated microphone sewn in, and rectangular flying goggles attached to the brow.

"What's going on?" I asked. "What are you doing?"

"What'ya' think I'm doin', Sonny? I'm gonna' go up there and take that sum-bitch down."

"What? *How?*"

He stopped his preparations just long enough to turn around and thump me in the chest. "I guess I'll just have ta' figure it out, now won't I?... *Ha!* In 'Nam we flew through anti-aircraft fire so thick it was like flyin' in a hailstorm! Before breakfast! We flew hundreds of missions! Dust-off chopper pilots," he said, thrusting his thumb up at his own face. "That was *us*—pickin' up our wounded boys. They shot me once in the ass, but I was back flyin' the *next day*. Did two-and-a-half years in a POW camp in North Viet Nam, too. I think I can manage ta' take down one gawd-damned *balloon!* Now, stay outta the way!"

Elizabeth screamed, "No! No! Anything could happen! The pilot could detonate the bomb anyway! Even if he doesn't detonate it, it could still go off. There's probably a switch, a failsafe. Farok's like that!"

Waltrip's eyes widened. "What *bomb?*"

"Mr. Waltrip."

"Larry."

"Larry. There is probably a nuclear warhead aboard that balloon," Keyes said, slowly and carefully. "We believe that the pilot is going to fly to the stratosphere and detonate the nuke."

"Mr. Waltrip," I said.

"Larry."

"Larry. I've got to get to the capsule of that balloon, kill the pilot, and try to bring that thing down, but under control."

The wily old dude smiled a little.

"There's an atomic bomb aboard," I said. "They're going to detonate it at one hundred thousand feet. And we have reason to believe that's just the start."

Waltrip chuckled. "Now, I'm here to say: I can get you up there, but there's only one way to get on."

"Parachute."

"You'll never make it. You must not be much of a parachutist or you'd know that. Besides, the only chutes I've got are the old army clunkers. They're big and heavy and there's no way you could maneuver in close enough."

"What are you thinking?"

"Wing walk. I do it all the time. During the lean times, I've done all kinds of stuff, aerobatics, stunt flying, you name it. Hell, I've even strapped tourists who wanted to wing walk to a chair fixed to the upper wing. Makes'm feel real adventurous."

"So, you mean, you can get me onto the capsule

by flying into the wind? You go the same speed as the balloon?"

"You must have studied physics in a comic book."

"What?"

He shook his head. "No! That's nuts!"

"But how do I get on?"

"There's but one way I can get you aboard that capsule. It's the Hammerhead Turn. I fly above the balloon, dive down below it to get up some speed, then fly vertically up until I stop, right next to the balloon. The skill involved is timing the ascent so that the airplane comes to a full stop right beside the capsule. It'll be absolutely still for just one second and you'll have to jump."

"What about the rope? Could I grab the rope?"

"What rope?"

"The rope hanging down from the capsule."

"Well, if there's a rope hanging down, it's not complete suicide. The other method—the one I was just telling you about, you know, saying you'd just jump off?"

"Uh huh."

"You wouldn't have made that."

"What?"

"Yep, I was just humoring you. But even somebody like *you* can grab a rope... I *guess*." He reached over and squeezed my biceps muscles. "Walking on the wing is tricky. It takes a lot of strength to hold on to the struts between the wings."

"And I can wear a parachute."

"You can, but I wouldn't advise it. The parachutes I have are army surplus. They're heavy as hell and bulky and they restrict your movement. To grab that rope, you'll have to be like a cat."

"But you do have a parachute, right?"

"Yep. There's one over there." He pointed to a green backpack laying in the corner of the hangar.

I looked at Keyes and Jakjak. "What do you think?"

"What choice do we have?" Keyes said.

Waltrip started climbing into the plane. "Y'all gonna stand there cuttin' bait or's somebody goin' fishin' with me? That balloon goes up at about 6-to-800 feet per minute." Waltrip settled into the cockpit and started flipping switches. "This Stearman goes up at 1600 feet per minute. If we leave right now we can just barely catch'em before they get to 13,000 feet, which is as high as this thing will go. If we wait one more minute they're going to be out of reach by the time we get up there."

Jakjak ran to the corner of the hangar and grabbed the parachute. We heard the battery whine inside the old biplane and the engine coughed a big cloud of black smoke and then started chugging. Suddenly it was like we were in a tornado, with the wind blasting backward from the propeller.

I quickly climbed into the leg loops of the parachute harness, which was heavy and confining, just as Waltrip had said. Jakjak handed me his 9mm, and yelled over the engine noise, "Dokte! Two shots left!"

"Hey! Greenhorn!" Waltrip yelled over the noise and wind. "Get in!"

I climbed aboard and before I was even sitting we were taxiing out to the main runway.

I sat, and Waltrip handed me a headset, which I put on. He immediately started talking, fast.

Chapter 41

Stearman Biplane
Runway 23/5
Elkins Regional Airport
5:56 a.m.

"THE HIGHER THE BALLOON gets, the faster it goes up. Once it gets above, say, 12,000 feet, it'll start going up at about 1,000 feet per minute. To get you on the capsule I have to do the Hammerhead with you as far out on the wing tip as you can get. It's tricky. The turbulence at this time of the year can be pretty strong. Also, I've never done this before."

I turned around in my seat to look back at him. "What?"

"I've never done a Hammerhead at 10,000 feet. The air's too damned thin up there. And I've never done one with some idiot hangin' way out there on my wing tip, either."

"But you think you can do it, right?"

"Well, now, there are few problems with the Hammerhead. First of all, the climb to 10,000 feet will take a bunch'a fuel. Secondly, taking the plane straight up in the Hammerhead uses up even more fuel, I mean a lot of fuel. If I could do it four or five times, I'd guarantee I could get it right, but I don't think I can do it more than twice and have enough fuel to get back home. Also, like I said, the air's real thin up there. Aerobatics in a slow-moving plane like this one can get kind'a, you know, *wild*."

I yelled into the microphone of my headset, "What do you mean, *wild*?"

"I mean we could go into a tail slide if I try to hold the airplane at the vertical position more than a second or two. The plane literally moves backward. It falls out of the sky. All kinds of things can happen if we tail slide. The rudder or the elevators can get pushed into a full deflection position or they can be ripped off or jammed, which makes it virtually impossible to control the airplane. The tail feathers on this bird aren't equipped to take the full pressure of a tail slide."

"So how do you avoid the tail slide?"

"By not waiting too long. If all goes well, the propeller will make the plane rotate 180 degrees straight down and gravity will do the rest. That is ... as long as the tail doesn't hit the capsule ... or sump'm else."

"Oh shit," I said.

"It'll work, maybe. It's *theoretically* possible, anyhow."

I turned around to look at him again. "You sounded a lot more sure of yourself on the ground!"

"Shit, man, I'm seventy-two years old. I've owned

that airport for forty years. I've done just about everything that can possibly be done in a flying machine, and I can do this, too."

I turned around and looked up at the balloon. It seemed to be in wrong place. "What's going on with the balloon?"

"Surface winds today are west-southwest, but up here there more southwest. With these upper-level winds, they'll go on a more northerly course, toward Gettysburg, or so I calculate."

My heart jumped. The Gettysburg Address was nomenclature in the decrypted messages. I clutched my chest. It seemed like the last straw. They were going to go through with it and they had planned well.

What was I getting into? I was the last line of defense. Me. A lump came to my throat as I thought of the dangers ahead of me. I thought of those I'd leave behind if I died, my precious boys, Mom, and of course the woman I wanted so much to marry.

Stearman Biplane
6500 Feet Over Elkins, West Virginia
5:58 a.m.

THE ENGINE NOISE AND wind were immense. It all seemed frantic. I had to concentrate. I had to think of my goal, my mission, and every contingency. I had to get my concentration right. I had to think like I do in surgery. I had to draw on every region of my mind, to focus, like I'd done in thousands of surgical procedures where every tiny millimeter—every tiny slice of human tissue—was of paramount importance.

I settled myself, centered my thoughts, and began to think through the procedure, to visualize the steps. All at once, the surreal nature of what I was doing and the events of the previous weeks vanished and I came to my senses. I spoke to Waltrip through the microphone: "Have you ever dealt with this kind of balloon? How do I get it down? How do these things work?"

"There should be a twist valve that allows you to vent gas through the top of the balloon. The valve should be within reach of the top of the capsule. They usually put one on the outside to help'em control the gassing of the balloon. You should be able to let some of the helium out that way. Most of 'em are like that. Also, the extra weight will help. With your body weight aboard and a little less helium—that should bring it slowly down."

"What about the capsule? Is the door locked from the inside?"

"It depends. The capsule in a high-altitude balloon is closed all around and of course it's pressurized inside. Ever since the Apollo fire in the Sixties, they've designed'em to be opened from both the inside and the outside. But I don't know anything about this one. They're all built one at a time, so who knows how they've sealed the hatch on this one? But I think you can do what you need to do on top of the capsule."

"No. I've got to get to the pilot. I've got to kill him or knock him out or something. He's sitting in there waiting to get to the right altitude. If he knows he's going down he might just pull the trigger on the bomb."

"Or he may climb out and throw you off. If he really

wants to get to the stratosphere, all he has to do is close the vent and if he's got some spare helium on board, he can start going up again."

"That's it. I've got to make him believe that he can still go up to the altitude he needs, and when he comes out, I'll kick his ass!"

"I bet you could do it. You're a pretty big fella."

"I'll shoot him if I have to."

"For God's sake, make sure you only shoot the *guy*. If you shoot a hole in the balloon you won't be able to control your fall. You can always close the vent if you're coming down too fast, but if you put a hole in that balloon, it'll probably grow. Once that happens, you'll fall out of the sky so fast your head'll spin. That is — before you go splat on the ground."

"Any tricks to walking on the wing?"

"Hand walk around the support struts between the wings, and reach for the N strut close to the end. When we get to the top of the Hammerhead Turn, you'll know."

"How will I know?"

"Because everything'll suddenly go quiet. Real quiet. It'll be like we're standing still."

Chapter 42

Stearman Biplane
12,000 Feet Above Ground Level
6:04 a.m.

THE BALLOON AND ITS capsule hung in the clear sky like an inverted teardrop. From our perspective in the approaching Stearman, it didn't appear to be going up or down. It seemed weightless, like a particle of dust hanging in an airless room. Around it there was nothing, no mountains in the background, no frame of reference, nothing, just open sky and a huge silver balloon.

I gulped. It didn't matter that I had a parachute. It didn't matter that other people wing walk. It looked impossible.

Suddenly Waltrip yelled into the headset and I jumped. "Okay! This is it! The balloon's higher than I'd expected, 12,000 feet. It'll take everything this old airplane's got to make a Hammerhead up here. We've got to go right now! Climb out of the cockpit and walk to the N strut on the right wing! Hang on, it will be hard to breathe because we're going so fast and the air's so thin. I'm going to climb 400 feet above the balloon, then dive to pick up speed. I'll be going 180 miles an hour at the bottom of the dive, and then I'll pull her straight up. The speed will go down quickly with the vertical climb, and as we decelerate, you'll have about one second at most to grab the rope. As soon as you let go of the strut, gravity will try to pull you down. Your timing has to be perfect. I'll try to have your wing tip at the rope when we reach zero speed. When I tell you to get off, do it immediately. If I miss, just hang onto the strut for dear life because going down after the turn will be even worse than going up."

As Waltrip started his climb, I saw the balloon going farther and farther under us.

I took off my headset and crawled out of the cockpit, onto the lower wing. My clothing flew into a frenzy, flapping wildly, and my face flattened. Holding onto the wood and wire was all I could think of. I was crouched over like an ape, trying to pick my way through the wires and struts. Every handhold felt like the end of the world, like it was the only thing I'd ever held onto in all my life, and the parachute rig was almost impossible to cope with in the confined space.

I heard Waltrip yell, "Faster!"

I reached the N strut at the end of the wing and made the mistake of looking down. It was awful. The feeling of open space was incredible. All that harrowing, falling, gravity—and death—exploded in my veins as a surge of nauseating adrenaline. Then Waltrip shouted, "Hold on to your britches! WE'RE GOING DOWN!"

Suddenly the plane dropped. We dove hard. I was looking straight down at the thousands and thousands of feet below me. The wind noise around me exploded as we accelerated. My footing gave way and I lost my ability to breathe completely. The steep dive made me feel like I was on a roller coaster. I could feel myself becoming lighter and lighter as we fell, like there was no way to stay on, like I was going to simply fly away from the wing.

Then the dive bottomed out and we began our climb. I had to cling to the strut with every ounce of strength I had.

The forces straining against me began to ease. Then they eased some more. The plane was moving slowly, then almost stopped. I looked to see the capsule still fifteen feet above. We weren't going to make it. The plane was pointing straight up and we were stopped in mid air, weightless.

The wind stopped. The rope was still five feet above me. It seemed to be slinging little black pellets from an old bag, harmlessly, into the air.

"WE MISSED!" Waltrip screamed. The plane turned over and dropped. "HOLD ON TO THAT STRUT!"

The wind exploded all around me and I was clinging to the wooden strut and gritting my teeth, fighting the forces trying to tear me from the plane.

We came out of the dive and I had a moment to think. I'd never make it with the parachute on my back. Waltrip was right. There was no way. There were too many forces at work here. Strangely, I felt a surge of confidence. *I can do this, but I've got to commit to doing it right.* I reached up and pulled the release on the harness and wriggled out of the parachute rig and let it fall. It shrank, and shrank, and shrank, and shrank, and it just kept tumbling, and tumbling, and then it was gone, lost in a 12,000-foot fall.

"NOW YOU'RE TALKIN!" I heard Waltrip shout.

"MOVE YOUR ASS, LARRY! GET ME UP THERE!"

"YOU GOT IT! I'VE GOT JUST ENOUGH FUEL FOR ONE MORE!"

My stomach sank again as we went into the dive. The wind accelerated all around me. We reached the bottom and started climbing up. I felt my legs straining against the G forces. The plane was pointing straight up, completely vertical. I held onto the N strut with all my strength. We were directly under the capsule and going upward. We were fifteen feet away and the plane was slowing. We were ten feet away. Six feet away. Almost there. The plane was slowing quickly. We were moving at crawl speed. My heart raced. This had to be it. Then it was there. The rope. The plane stopped completely. Everything was still.

"GRAB THAT ROPE!" Waltrip shouted.

I hesitated for a moment as the plane began to drop. Now or never! I let go of the plane with one hand and grabbed the rope with the other. The plane dropped behind me. The engine noise fell away and I was there in total silence, alone, hanging by one hand in the open sky.

Chapter 43

Stearman Biplane
12,500 Feet Above Ground Level
6:06 a.m.

WALTRIP SMILED FOR A moment. The airspeed indicator was at zero. Then he felt the plane sliding backward. "Holy shit," he said.

It was one second too late. The joystick smashed backward into his crotch. The backward motion had slammed the elevator to its full travel, ramming the stick into him. Stars flashed before his eyes. The intense pain knocked him senseless. He felt weightless as the Stearman slid awkwardly backward, a bird with useless wings.

He'd been a flight instructor too long and knew the danger. But the pain in his crotch paralyzed him. He couldn't see or move. The Stearman fell vertically downward, tail first.

The Capsule
6:19 a.m.

I TOOK DEEP BREATHS to regain my strength, but it did little good. The air was very thin. I looked around. I took several deep breaths and reached up with my other hand and grasped the rope. I knew my arms would fail within just a few minutes. I had to get to the capsule quickly.

I pulled myself upward with extreme difficulty. I needed to travel just ten precious feet. I tried instinctively to get a foothold, kicking my legs, but there was nothing under me but thousands of feet of open space. *Please, arms. Please, just pull. Just pull up a little. Don't fail me.*

I pulled myself up about halfway, but already I was tiring. My grip was slipping, no matter how hard I squeezed. I was only going up a few inches with each pull, but I was also sliding down. I was panting and my arms were on fire and on their way to failing. *Come on, Scott, you can do this. All those years of working out with heavy weights. All those years of playing sports. You can do this. One more pull. One more.*

I took four gulps of thin air, which didn't seem to do any good, and pulled again. I clamped my knees around the rope and pushed upward and my head bumped the bottom of the capsule. I looked frantically for some sort of handhold on the side of the slick, egg-shaped, fiberglass shell. There was one at the top of the hatch, but it was too far away. But there was one thing I could do. My foot slid, very slowly upward, until it rested on the latch of the capsule's door. Then I kicked as hard as I could.

I slid up, up, up, and then was on top, still clinging to

the rope in my hands. I took more deep breaths and pulled my feet up. I rested for a few seconds before reaching up to the cables that connected the capsule to the balloon. With great effort, I pulled myself up to stand. I struggled to put my weight on my legs. They held. I was standing.

With the balloon moving at the same speed as the wind, I felt no resistance, nothing like I'd anticipated. I was standing on top of the capsule. I couldn't believe it.

In The Stearman
6:20 a.m.

WALTRIP WAS IN AGONIZING pain, but he needed to act. Gravity would make the nose follow through with the maneuver but maybe not until the elevator or the rudder had been too damaged to control the airplane. He grabbed the stick with both hands and tried to push and hold it in a neutral position to give the old biplane the best chance to survive. *If any plane can take this pressure,* he thought, *it's my Stearman.* He knew the only chance he had now was the gravitational pull on the heavy front end of the plane. Would the nose drop straight down before something really broke?

On The Capsule
6:21 a.m.

I WAS TIRED, MORE tired than I'd ever been in my life. It took a lot of energy just to stand erect. I had to sit. I let go of my vice-like grasp on the cables and lowered my body until my butt rested on the top of the capsule. I gasped for oxygen. *If the pilot knows we're starting to descend, he'll come up here after me.* I had to have a plan.

In The Biplane
6:23 a.m.

FOR A MOMENT, WALTRIP felt panic. As his head cleared, the airplane seemed to take forever to reverse direction and become a flying machine once again instead of a cinder block. A thousand things went through his head. He thought of his wife, Pat. His life insurance would more than pay his existing debts for the airport repairs of the past couple of years, leaving intact a handsome nest egg for her. His kids? They were all grown and successful in their work. His employees? Someone would buy the airport at a good price and keep them on the payroll. So who did he have left to worry about? *Me*, he thought. *I want to keep living and keep flying for many years.*

On The Capsule
6:24 a.m.

I LOOKED OVER THE side and located the hatch. But I was a little late. The door was already opening. I got to my knees and positioned myself securely between the cables.

A high-altitude helmet, covering a large man's head, slowly emerged from the hatchway of the capsule. The tinted face shield and oxygen tubes made him look like a large insect. He'd felt something, obviously, but at that point I assumed he didn't know exactly what was

The Encryption Game

happening. I kept myself out of sight and hoped I was right.

I took deep breaths. That, and the adrenaline pumping in my body, gave me a little strength. But I still felt short of breath. The balloon was going up fast now. The atmosphere was getting noticeably thinner. I was still unsure about what to do. Only a few hours before, I'd been eating dinner. Now, it occurred to me, grimly, that I suddenly found myself in a cage match, one of those bare handed fights in confined spaces. There was nowhere to go. Wrapping one hand around the connecting cables over my head, I prepared myself. *The pistol*, I thought to myself, *I have to use it*. I reached into my pocket.

The suited pilot reached up for a handhold above the hatch, then hoisted himself to the top of the capsule. It was clear then that he'd seen me. I raised the gun and fired directly into his face shield. The glass shattered and the pressurized air inside his suit vented with a sudden moan and through the jagged shards I saw the pilot's face for the first time.

Emmanuel.

It was the man I'd shot in Williamsburg. Emmanuel. Farok's man. He was a terrorist, and at last I had him. A small trickle of blood was oozing from a hole in his cheek. My first instinct was that I had to hold on to this man, somehow. I had to produce him in a court of law, or bring him to the CIA, or to anybody who'd listen to me. And in that moment of hesitation, he reached out and pinned my hand and the gun against my chest. I could see his wicked smile inside his helmet. He raised his hand to push me off the capsule and into space. I struggled to free my hand and the pistol. He was big and strong and he was forcing me over the side. I could feel myself becoming helpless without adequate oxygen. With my free hand I drew back and delivered a punch to his mid-section. I threw another one. I hammered away at his stomach. But the layers of heavy plastic of his suit acted as padding. Even just that small amount of effort at that altitude wore me out. He planted his feet firmly on the capsule and pushed me toward the edge. I shoved his hands up in the air and hit him again, solidly, in his stomach. He groaned, then punched at me. I shoved his hands to the side and hit him again. I heard him growl like an animal. He was starting to gasp for air, like I was. He brought his knee up to my stomach and it solidly hit his intended target. It hurt something awful, but there wasn't a second to cry out. I hooked my leg around his knee and shoved. It caught him off balance. He grabbed at the cables to keep from falling. He came back at me. He stomped my foot and held it, setting me up for blows to my chest. I was hurt. I felt blood come into my mouth. As a doctor, I knew his ribs would be his most vulnerable spot, if only I could get the right angle on him. He turned very slightly to one side and I saw my chance. There weren't any portals or hardware on the sides of the suit, just plastic sheeting. I slammed my fist into his ribs. He screamed out, then staggered. I knew I had him. His knees buckled. I had to hold onto this man. I didn't want him to go over the side. I didn't want him to die. I wanted him alive. I slammed blows into his ribs. He was coughing violently. I was punching and punching and blood was streaming out of his mouth. I pounded his unprotected side, and then, at last, he fell. His body dropped back, and I knew he was out.

I was gasping for air. I needed oxygen. I was shivering now from the extreme cold. My body trembled. I felt more blood in my throat. Consciousness waned. I flopped to my butt and wrapped both my arms around Emmanuel. *I can't let him slip off this capsule*, I thought. *I need his intact body for my trial, if I live.*

I pulled up the rope that I'd climbed on earlier and threw it around Emmanuel's body, then hurriedly lashed him to the cables at the top of the capsule. But I was fading. I couldn't breathe and I felt that dreadful feeling when you are deeply cold and there is no way to get warm. I had to reach the helium valve, now, or I, too, would be finished.

But where was it? I frantically looked everywhere. What did Waltrip say? *Above* the capsule? I looked up. There, above my head, was a red handle, like the cut off for a large gas main. I reached to the valve to turn it off. But it didn't budge. I tried again. Nothing. I tried to inhale oxygen but it seemed pointless. There was no air now. Ten minutes had passed since I'd stepped off of Waltrip's plane. We had to be somewhere near 23,000 feet and going up at perhaps as much as a thousand feet every minute. I had maybe two-to-three minutes left before hypothermia and loss of oxygen overcame me. My hands were already frostbitten and becoming useless. I tried again. It was stuck, probably frozen. I was on my own. I had to close that valve. I took two deep breaths and then pulled with all my might until my chest had risen to the valve. I was trembling like a leaf, holding on, grunting in extreme effort.

And then it twisted. It moved! I pulled rhythmically,

grunting and crying out. I took another breath and yelled out and it twisted again. The valve opened! The handle was down! I had no idea if gas was leaking out because the opening was at the top of the balloon, a hundred feet above me. But the handle was down. There was nothing more I could do. I slumped to the top of the capsule. I gasped to breathe and I thought of Scotty and Jeremy, and of dear Elizabeth. I could not move. Then, there was nothing.

Chapter 44

In The Biplane
6:25 a.m.

THE ALTIMETER SHOWED A rapid fall. Waltrip was at eleven thousand feet. The plane was beginning to turn. The nose was moving down. The 450 HP engine was roaring defiance despite the mistreatment. Waltrip gingerly moved the stick, praying that there were still elevators on the airplane to respond. The nose was down so he pulled the throttle back to idle to reduce the forces and gently started pulling back. After what seemed an eternity, the plane began to lift. He took a deep breath and steadied his hands on the controls. He was flying again.

Landing Strip
Elkins Airport
6:41 a.m.

WALTRIP'S PLANE ROLLED TO a stop in front of the fuel station. Elizabeth and Jakjak ran to meet him.

Waltrip started talking the moment the engine coughed to a stop. "If he's successful, that balloon will land out in the boonies somewhere."

Waltrip got out and ran to his office. He was back in one minute, huffing and puffing from his sprint. "Take this," he said to Jakjak, handing him a handheld VHF radio. "I'm about to break about ten laws concerning aviation radio traffic, but in this case a man's life is at stake."

"What do you have in mind?" Keyes asked.

"I'm going to refuel. You two set out in that car of yours. I'll head in the direction of the balloon. We'll maintain contact via the radios. If I spot it, I'll call."

"What about radar? Can't we just track them on radar?"

"We can, but that won't put us on the scene when that thing comes down. It helps to have people on the ground when an aircraft like that lands. It needs people under it to help the pilots. They'll probably need first aid or transport to a hospital. No. It's better to pursue. It's better to chase it."

"Which way should we head?"

"The air mass is pretty calm today. They're probably moving slowly. How far up they went, I don't know, but if I had to guess at it, I would say they will end up somewhere between thirty and fifty miles east-northeast from here. Go up Highway 220, toward Moorefield. If he succeeded in getting that balloon to release some gas, we should be able to spot him coming down."

Chapter 45

In The Stearman
7:20 a.m.

WALTRIP RETRACED THE FLIGHT to where he last saw the balloon, and then continued on the course of the prevailing wind. After fifteen minutes, he saw it, at five thousand feet. As he closed in on the silver aircraft, he saw that two bodies lay on top of the capsule.

Inside the Lotus, Jakjak's radio crackled with Waltrip's voice: "I've spotted them. They're right where I thought they'd be, but they're too low. They're coming down too fast. There is a second man on top. It's the pilot. They're both lying there. It looks to me like they're both unconscious. They may be dead. The balloon's falling too fast. It'll crash pretty hard. If they're not dead already, the landing might kill'em."

"Where do you tink de weel land?"

"Other side of Moorefield. Can't tell you the exact spot yet."

Keyes pulled out her cell phone without taking her eyes off the road. "Okay, that's it. I'm calling the cops." She turned the phone on and saw on the screen, "54 Missed Calls." Before she could dial, another call came in. It was Perkins' number, the same one as all the other "Missed Calls." "Perkins, Scott's bringing the balloon down. I don't know how he did it, but it's coming down near Moorefield, West Virginia. This is a Farok job all the way. Call everyone you know and get us some help out here—"

"What the hell is going on! I've been calling you guys—"

Before he could finish, she hung up the phone and dialed 911. Cool as a cucumber, she said, "I want to report a ballooning accident near Moorefield, on Highway 220. We need everything, police, fire, EMT, everything you've got."

"I tink we already gawt some help, Mademoiselle," Jakjak said, looking back.

The racing Evora had obviously attracted some attention.

Highway 220
7:20 a.m.

TWO STATE TROOPER PATROL cars were now matching speed with the flying Lotus. It was only a matter of time before

The Encryption Game

more would appear, but in front.

The radio crackled with Waltrip's voice once again: "You've got a caravan of cops behind you. Take your next left. That will put you in the general vicinity."

The Evora skidded through a wild left turn and Jakjak felt himself thrown violently against the passenger door, then Keyes stomped on the gas.

The balloon was now only a quarter of a mile away, but the perspective from the Lotus was misleading. It was coming down fast, but nevertheless its descent appeared to be quite slow. The radio crackled again, "They're going to go down in the Potomac. They're going to land in the river."

Keyes slammed on the brakes and threw open the door. Suddenly she and Jakjak were in a sprint across an open field. They could hear the patrol cars skidding to a halt behind them and sirens coming from every direction.

A tree line lay ahead of them and on the other side of that, the Potomac River. The balloon, the big, silver, inverted teardrop, with its capsule hanging underneath, was now only a hundred feet above the ground. It was the first time that either Jakjak or Keyes had been close enough to the aircraft to appreciate the enormity of the thing. It was huge, a hundred feet tall and majestic. It came down in a stately fashion, descending out of the sky as though on autopilot, heading right for the river.

Jakjak passed Keyes and crashed wildly through the underbrush near the tree line, yelling "Dokte! Dokte!"

The capsule disappeared for a moment, passing on the far side of the trees. Just as Jakjak burst through the tree line he saw the capsule hit the water with a splash. The balloon, suddenly relieved of all its weight and buoyed by the recoil of the egg-shaped craft hitting the water, lifted off and flew again. It flew in a low arc and then hit the river again. The whole aircraft was now like a huge beach ball, rising a few feet and settling down gently.

Jakjak flung himself into the muddy brown water of the Potomac and began swimming frantically. Keyes burst through the trees and she, too, hurled herself into the river with a splash. The capsule hit for a third time and rolled hard, dumping Scott James off of the top. His body splashed into the water, face down.

The current was taking the whole thing downstream, and Jakjak and Keyes were swimming in the cold water as hard as they could. James' body showed no reaction. Keyes reached him and turned him over. "Scott! Scott!" She shook him, trying to get him to wake up. "Scott!"

In textbook fashion, Keyes turned his torso around so that his back was facing her, grasped his body in one arm, and began backstroking toward the shore with the other. "Grab that son-of-a-bitch," she screamed to Jakjak, "and make sure he doesn't go anywhere!"

"I got heem!" Jakjak called over his shoulder as he struggled up the side of the floating capsule.

At the shore, Keyes was met by a swarm of first responders. Two EMTs took James and positioned an oxygen mask on his face. He began to cough, faintly, and to spew foam. More and more, the shore of the Potomac looked like a military operation. News crews began pulling up. A helicopter started circling. Elizabeth stayed with Scott James, holding him tightly.

Chapter 46

Day 20
Grant Memorial Hospital
9:00 a.m.

I AWAKENED. I DIDN'T know what had happened over the previous three days. They say I was in and out of consciousness, but I don't remember any of it.

I looked up and saw Elizabeth. I tried to smile, but my face didn't move much. First, Elizabeth kissed me, then Jakjak stood over me and smiled.

I saw Jakjak's lips moving, and heard his words, "Dokte, that was one helluva ride you took. De FBI has Emmanuel in custody."

"Jakjak?"

"It's me alright, Dokte."

I reached and squeezed his arm. "Keep talking like that, but remind me every now and then that it's really you saying those words."

The kids were all over the bed, hugging me.

The doctors called my condition hypoxic encephalopathy, due to a combination of the low atmospheric pressure, extreme fatigue, extreme cold, and marked hypoxia. That's where the blood in my lungs came from. I was afraid when I saw it spewed on the capsule that I was experiencing the bends, but the doctors said no. They said my condition would affect my mental state, but in a week or so I'd have complete cerebral recovery.

They say Perkins was my first visitor, although apparently I was unconscious when he came. It was reassuring that he'd taken the time and effort to come all the way to see me. The nurses told me that Elizabeth never left my side.

As soon as I was back to myself, I was back to being interrogated again, although the various agencies referred to it as being "interviewed." I was of course asked about the terrorists, and Elizabeth told me that there was, indeed, a nuke on that balloon. But Perkins and his group saw to it that the miniature bomb was kept secret, and in fact, it was never revealed to the public that there was ever a live nuke anywhere over American skies. The story that circulated was that a terrorist had kidnapped me and was transporting me to Canada.

Emmanuel was taken alive, but to an "undisclosed location." That remains a can of worms. Perkins and perhaps other unknown players were able to have the case of capital murder dismissed. But the identity of who shot Malcolm Johnson remains a mystery. There have been delays in this matter, nothing but delays. The Justice Department responded to my questions by giving some bullshit story that the evidence in my case was protected by national security concerns. My fear is that the public will never see the ballistics, never see the Kevlar vest Emmanuel was wearing or the .45 slug that killed Malcolm Johnson. Johnson's own family has begun to inquire, which is the best thing that could happen, because you know what happened when I asked too many questions? They called me "Oswald," as in Lee Harvey.

I believe this thing is only going to get worse. I believe that Josh Edwards was murdered, and that the films of the shooting in Williamsburg were tampered with. I have debated with myself a hundred times whether or not I should just go straight to the media and start talking. This would violate my pact with the freak who came to my jail cell. If he is indeed helping me, I do not know. Regardless, I remain the guiltiest man in America. As far as the public is concerned, a shot was fired by me, and a good man was killed.

The ISIS cell in Gettysburg was discovered, but the tactic of using the refugees to bring in terrorists was discounted. The thirty they arrested were already in America when the refugees arrived, or so the news anchors were told.

There was no terrorist cell discovered in The Naval Base at Cape May, the only other group that Keyes was able to identify through her decryption efforts. Just one man was arrested. His computers revealed none of his contacts. Even with our argument that he was probably communicating through WhatsApp or Signal or one of the others, and that he was probably able to erase everything, completely, seemed to meet with no response. He was presumed to be a "lone wolf."

After my release from the hospital, Elizabeth and I stayed in Gettysburg for the night. I wanted to ask her to marry me, which I had been planning to do for quite a while, but the time didn't seem right. One thing we did discuss, though: We must kill or capture Omar Farok, or our lives will never be at peace. Which is all I want. I just want to go back to the way things were. I want to start a center for plastic surgery, with Elizabeth working near me all the time.

We decided that night that we must go to Italy as soon as possible. Simply put, there have been too many messages about the Vatican circulating in Farok's organization to ignore—too many connections. Elizabeth said she knows where to start looking and that Farok would never expect us to show up there. She said it would give us the element of surprise. I talked to Mom and the kids about going to Vatican City, and they loved the idea. There is no way I'm letting them out of my sight, come what may.

But I am a free man, at least for the time being, and I'm pretty sure there won't be any ballooning madness in Italy. That's a relief. I'm actually looking forward to it. Scotty, "The Cipher King," says he wants to go to Venice while we are there, "before it falls into the sea."

Also by Glenn Shepard

The Missile Game
The Zombie Game
The Ebola Game
The Vatican Game (December 2016)
Faces In A Bamboo Garden (2017)

Acknowledgements

My special thanks to John Haslett for all his efforts in pulling my books together (and selling them), to Annie Biggs, for her editorial assistance and cover designs, and to Richard Krevolin for his continued support and friendship. Tim McSwain (JD, ATP, CF II, Aviation Consultant) does an exciting hammerhead. Thanks to him for taking me on one of the wildest, most exciting (and scary) rides I've ever been on, and for his legal direction of the court proceedings. Barbara Deyoung connected me to Anonymous, a valuable group in our fight against ISIS. And, as always, thanks to sons Barclay, my computer guru, and Glenn Jr., who is destined to be the famous writer in the family.

Made in the USA
San Bernardino, CA
04 May 2018